Adair Welcker

Romer, King of Norway, and Other Dramas

.

Adair Welcker

Romer, King of Norway, and Other Dramas

ISBN/EAN: 9783744787772

Printed in Europe, USA, Canada, Australia, Japan

Cover: Foto ©Andreas Hilbeck / pixelio.de

More available books at **www.hansebooks.com**

ROMER, KING OF NORWAY,

AND

OTHER DRAMAS.

BY

ADAIR WELCKER.

SACRAMENTO:
PRESS OF LEWIS & JOHNSTON.
1885.

☞ NOTICE.—These books will be sent by the writer, postage pre-
paid, to any address, upon the receipt, by postal note or otherwise,
of 75 cents; and when five or more copies are ordered, will be sent
to booksellers for 50 cents per copy. ☜

PREFACE.

THESE works are placed in book form, in order that
the people of a future age may have the opportunity
to open their mouths with wonder, at the utterances of a
very ordinary dead man; and that commentators in that
day may have a method of making a living. If what so
many say of these works is true, this must be the result.

The Preface is written for the benefit of that large por-
tion of mankind who are led by the nose in making their
judgments; and for those who, upon reading this remark,
will swear that they are not to be so led.

The plays are written for the few in this age who are too
great for prejudice; and for the people of an age in the
future, when the past is not envied:—when envy of the
writer shall have ceased with his death. As it is an unpar-

donable crime against the vast mass of men for one person
in his own lifetime, to excel the rest in anything, although
others will excel him in other respects, I expect to meet
with strong condemnatiom for these works.   So let it be—
it is the law of nature.

As for myself, I believe that my experience in the world
has freed me from the effects of condemnation—has cured
me of a care for praise; for I know that both are as often
misplaced as they are justly bestowed.   Were commenda-
tion to be bestowed upon the dramas, it would be but the
repetition of an old story; for one of them has been printed
in pamphlet form for six years, another for three, and during that time they have been read by many persons, and
have been, by almost as many, pronounced to be of the
highest form of literature.

By a strange unanimity of opinion, they have been pronounced to be made of the same material as the writings of
the greatest of dramatists.

As for censure, if it be bestowed upon the works, and

they cannot stand it, let them die; and if it is bestowed upon myself, I can stand it; for as I have said before, the hour is passed when I could have been affected by the world's censure or its blame; and whether the judgments of the world are various, or unanimous; for, or against, I am satisfied.

The works, however, are written for another purpose. Whatever their merits, or demerits they have in them some of those sentiments that belong to our race; and the humble hope of the writer is that they have been put into such a shape that they will take part against wrong and wage war for the right—for this should be the end and aim of all writing.

Sacramento, Cal. ADAIR WELCKER.

THE BITTER END.

THE BITTER END.

A DRAMA.

ACT I.

Scene I.—A little garden in the rear of a neat but small cottage, in San Francisco. The cottage L. C. in the background. A gate R. C. that opens upon a pathway that leads round to the front. A door C. opening into the back part of the house.

LILY and JOSEPHINE discovered.

Lily. Yes, Josephine, my kindest, dearest friend,
Misfortunes came like birds of prey upon us.
First came my brother's death. When last I saw thee,
We little thought he'd take so soon the wings
Of Death, and fly away to Heaven.

Jos.   Ah, Lily!
My poor, poor friend; my heart is bleeding for thee!

Lily. The burning fever first did scorch his brow;
Then sickness racked him with her cruel pains;—
I hear him now, with his poor, piteous wail,
Call out for help, in his delirium.
A soothing sleep at last drove off his pain,
And while he slept, all stood around his bed
With anxious faces, waiting till he waked.

And then he ope'd his eyes, and smiled on us,
And ask'd that we would raise him up, and then
He sang a hymn, and said good by, and died.

   Jos.   Oh, Lily! Lily! I know 'tis hard—'tis very hard!
It seems a ruling of some power beyond us
That woe shall follow woe.
But Lily, look you up; this nature of ours
Being grandly harmonized, brings us oblivion
For all our woes when they are overpast.
And when to-day is grown a yesterday
New turned events dislodge these woes within us.

   Lily.   But often when my memories fly
Back to my childhood's home, like swallows that still seek
Their nests torn down by cruel Winter's storms.
Can I forget the old back stairs, where oft
My little brother's feet came, step by step?
The little room, where, watching his worn face,
We saw him die?   And then there was a vine
Where all the birds of Summer came to woo:
It was a honeysuckle vine, and oft
The sun's rays stealing came, through its soft leaves,
To wake me i' the morning.
                    [*Bell rings at front of the house.*
                         Who can it be?

   Jos.   My aunt,
To take me home.   But list!—yes, 'tis her voice.

   Mrs. Stone. [*within.*] This change to poverty robs them
      of life
And chills each germ of action.
Ha, now! not yet? but I will bring them up.
                         [*Rings violently.*

Jos. I know not why it is; my aunt does seem
To have a strange dislike for my sweet friend.
    Enter through gate R. C. MRS. STONE and BLACKWELL.
Mrs. Sto. Well, niece,
Did you grow weary while you waited for me?
Jos. No, aunt; here, with my friend, the fleeting hours
Were gilded o'er with golden happiness!
Mrs. Sto. A gentle friend, indeed! So sweet is she
That all the baby stars will press their faces
Against the windows in the vault of heaven,
To gaze down on her lovely innocence!
And I know one (thy cousin and my son),
Whose eyes were captured by her innocence:
He listens to her soft and cooing words,
Which chased each other out her snowy throat,
As soft and innocent as doves' notes are—
And all the world does know, the dove does coo
Only for innocence:
Black. Hell's innocence!
Jos. The mind swift to imagine guilt in others,
Is rotten in itself.
Mrs. Sto. Now stop that magpie chattering; come,
To our home.
Jos. Good by, sweet Lily, 'till we meet again.
Mrs. Sto. [*Aside to Blackwell.*] A tender morsel 'tis of
    pleasure, when
We have a power, that wand-like, we can wield
To make men tremble!—you make a waste of time—
Come Josephine!
            [Exeunt MRS. STONE, BLACKWELL and JOSEPHINE R. C.
Lily. And some there are whose lives are never at ease

Until they have the power to command.
One hath a frowning face to wither smiles ;
The other smiles—will they be withered ?

                    [*Exit through door* c. *into the house.*

Enter through gate R. C. MR. and MRS. ARDEN, and they
    sit together on a bench L. under some trees.

  Mrs. Ard. The little left of what we once did have
Is going fast ; soon will it all be gone—what then ?

  Ard. Ay, that I'd ask my wife—what then ?

  Mrs. Ard. I'll tell thee what ; then will starvation come,
And cling upon us 'till the flesh is gone.

  Ard. I've done my best to gain a livelihood ;
From morn to night have wandered round these streets ;
Asked oft for work, but did receive rebuffs,
And met cold looks, that silent insult bore ;
My clothes jeered at ; forgot by former friends
Who knew me well when I was prosperous.
Ah ! I have dragged through many a dreary day,
Until the heart did weary grow and sick,
And 'tlll I wished to lay me down and die,
Like some poor dog I've seen lie i' the gutter !
But then the thought of thee, and of my child,
Came to my mind, and urged me on again ;
And now, for this, you taunt me with the pain—
The poverty I've wrought—Oh ! 'tis too much !

  Mrs. Ard. I taunt thee ? No ! I cast no taunt at thee ;
But still, I think our daughter might have deigned
To drop her selfishness, and think of us,
But, like a queen that had a thousand fortunes,
She coldly did reject her lover,
Because, forsooth, she thought she ne'er could love him !

Ard. All this is strange—I never heard of this !—
And is it long that he hath woo'd my daughter ?
   Mrs. Ard. As long as Summer is, with Winter placed
    behind it,
Has he been wooing her beneath your eyes.
   Ard. I knew that, like another visitor,
A few short evenings had he spent with her.
   Mrs. Ard. Why, e'en as sure as came the night, of late,
This wooer came, and in our Lily's ear
Did whisper—but she put rough barriers there—
Yet still he poured his soft words in her ear
Until the hour grew late, and the poor lights
Did grow a-weary guarding off the dark.
But she had not an answer for this love,
In all her pride, and all her selfishness !
   Ard. Oh, wife! let not these thoughts arise in you.
Selfish, say you? A thought of selfishness
Ne'er dared to wander in her gentle heart!
And pride ? —Oh, think not that ! These hardships
Harden your thoughts. For sweetest natures
When chafing beneath the weight of heavy woes
Grow for the time unjust.
   Mrs. Ard. And he does give a golden reason for
His wooing !
   Ard. And would you make a bargain of our child ?
O, no, my wife ! When not oppressed by care,
You had not thought like this; and soon again,
When better times have brightened up before us,
Your thoughts will take again their former course.
   Mrs. Ard. When fortune comes, fools only will not know
How dainty are her favors.

But thus it is through all the length of life :
Fortune we use not when 'tis in our power,
And when it has escaped, we rue it's loss !
       [Enter LILY through house door c.]
Tell me now, Lily, why like you not your wooer ?
He has good looks—such looks had pleased me well,
When I was of your age—a manly form,
A gallant bearing, and a sparkling eye,
That speaks an unheard language, sweeter far
Than the soft-tongued nightingale could speak.
And he would give an ample fortune to you.
    Lily.   I have a reason that I may not give ;
A reason that would make me rather work
Until the flesh is worn from off these arms.
Before I would consent to be his bride !
    Ard.   Nor shall my darling, forced against her will,
Give up her hand to one she does not love,
While lives her father, with a breast so broad,
That it may yet brave off life's beating storms !
             [Exit ARDEN into the house c.
    Mrs. Ard.   Again, I ask, why can you love him not ?
    Lily.   And still, I say, I have a reason, mother,
That I would keep a prisoner in this brain,
Till death draws back the bolts to let it free !
    Mrs. Ard.   But I'm your mother, child; should not your
      secrets
Be known to me, as well as to yourself ?
    Lily.   Since, mother, then, you still wish that 1 should
Give you my secret; know that this man's mother,
Without a cause, has so insulted me,
Up to the top of all her malice !

With cruel, bitter sneers, hid in a smile.
At first she did insinuate that I
Was but a poor, low wretch, that sought, with wily arts,
To steal away th' affections of her son,
Who, though I did look coldly on his wooing,
Still will persist.

 Mrs. Ard. And I suppose that something she hath said,
Which, though her words no masked meanings bore,
Did so appear to your suspicious mind.

 Lily. Ah, yes, my mother, they bore meanings sharp
As knives, with which they pierced me to the heart !
At times, when she did say some bitter thing,
She smiled the while, with that hard, chilling smile,
That speaks in every tongue.
Ah, no; I cannot ever marry him,
For then she'd smile upon my very dreams !

 Mrs. Ard. If she's a woman, are you not another ?
Poor, timid thing, I fain must pity you ;
You were not made for such a world as this—

 Lily. I tell you mother, a bitter life's before me
If I should take his hand; none of life's joys
Will ever reach my heart; dark shadows only
Will fall from off the years that, like to trains
Of funerals, will slowly cross the heaven.
There is a voice deep down within my heart
Proclaims this doom to me. Whether this be
A spirit speaking with a voice from heaven,
I do not know; but know the voice speaks truth.
Tell me now, mother,
Shall I surrender up my hand to him ?

 Mrs. Ard. I am too old, my child, to be deceived

By these thy youthful fancies; since you ask
For my opinion, in such rounded terms,
Know that I would accept.
   Lily.   Mother, it shall be done!
   Mrs. Ard.   Lily, say not
Hereafter, that I have advised thee to it.
I only say, that I would marry him.   [*Exeunt.*

   SCENE II.—An open place in front of Mrs. Stone's house in Berkeley: the full moon rises over the hills.

Enter GODFREY, R.

   God.   Before the night came here was she to meet me;
Either some strange mischance hath fallen her,
Or else kind hearted Night has drawn her veil,
Before the time, to keep the hot-rayed sun
From off her face.   Now come the little stars;
Through every crack of heaven do they peep down
To catch a view of her o'er lovely face!
But now she comes! I hear her steps
Making sweet music for th' enraptured air!

Enter JOSEPHINE, L.

   Jos.   And did you think that I would never come?
   God.   The hours did truly seem stretched out so long,
I might have named them never; but since now
I see you here, the evil of that time
Does serve but as a contrast to these moments,
That, like to sunbeams, frightened by the night,
Do swiftly flee away!
   Jos.   I had been here,
But that some envious demon held me back,
Now placing this, now that, across my path!

God. 'Tis strange, then, that the mighty fairy legions
Sallied not forth to guard you 'gainst this demon ;
For I know that these fairies love you well ;—
I've seen them oft, wrapt in a cloak of sunbeams,
Coming, unknown to you, to steal sweet kisses
From off thy rosy lips ; at other times
Bearing the hue from off thy lovely cheek
To paint their home, the cloud-placed rainbow, with !
 Jos. You seem to be acquainted well with these
Same tiny beings from another world.
'Tis only through the gate of midnight dreams,
Be it now known, that we may enter in
The fairy kingdom.
 God. Speak you of dreams, my lovely Josephine ?
Then I tell you that has reality
Stamped on it's face. You know I've loved you long ;—
Deny it not with those hard frowns ; and yet
They are but masks and prove unnatural
On such a face as thine.
I've loved you long and well, and now I ask
A mighty boon indeed—your hand sweet one :—
No answer now ? Ah ! in thy eye I see
The hard word " No " look forth ; O, banish it
From that sweet place, where heretofore
Kind smiles alone a dwelling had !
 Jos. Perhaps it was not there ; or, if it was,
T'is banished.
In answering thus, it may have seemed that I
Have been too soon in so surrendering
My hand to you ; if so, this my excuse—
 God. You give excuse ? No, no, 'twere better far

To end all laws and customs.   Oh ! now is all
My happiness complete !

  Jos.   And in the center of this happiness
I'm forced to tear myself away from you !
But blessings rest
Within the thought we soon shall meet again !

  God.   O, go not yet ; the hour is not yet late !

  Jos.   Nay, but the moon is sinking o'er the hill ;
See how her poor, wan face looks thin and pale.
I wonder hath she lost some one of those
Her myriad, star-browed children, that
She weeps while she majestically moves
Through night's blue heaven ?

  God.   If she is weeping, then I'll pity her ;
For, while I feel the sweetness of thy love,
I cannot think but all the world is sad !

  Jos.   The tide of night hath nearly reached the top;
Now must I tear myself away from you,
For there is one who watches all my conduct,
Searching some place that slander may creep in
To bring me ruin.

  God.   But not yet, Josephine! the stars
That mark the minute places in the sky
Have not been three times rounded by the hand
Of silence that doth mark the hour of night !

  Jos.   Were I to mark the hours upon this clock,
The morning light would guide me to my home.

  God.   The hours of time have shorter grown of late.

  Jos.   Oh, Godfrey, would that I might yet remain !
But I must tear myself away from you !
Good by, my love, good by !   [Exit JOSEPHINE, R.

God. Gone ! And is she gone ? O, evening breeze,
Bear these my blessings after her.   [Exit GODFREY L.
          Enter L. MRS. STONE and BLACKWELL, cautiously.
Mrs. Sto. You have already sworn an oath so strong
That it would bind the fleeting clouds together,
And tie the winds from north and east and south,
Until the earth did rest in drowsy stillness !
Black. Aye, I am bound to bind up in this brain
Your every word, and ev'n your smallest whisper.
If this be not enough, I swear again—
Mrs. Sto. Nay, hush—
An' I had not a stronger hold on you,
I would not give an unsubstantial shadow
For all thy oaths.   But to the business—
You know the father of my niece is dead ?
Black. Of Josephine ?—aye, dead
As skeletons dead in the deep, dead sea !
Mrs. Sto. And more than this, you know her father had
A fortune that—
Black. He lost in speculation.
Mrs. Sto. No ; there's our point ; he never lost it.
But when he lay upon the bed of death,
Then, with his trembling hand he wrote his will,
And gave that will to me.
By its wording, I was executor :—
Her father died upon the Atlantic shore ;
Some relatives she still hath living there,
Of whom she knows not, nor shall ever know
While thought burns in this brain.
Black. [*aside.*]   There thought will dwell,

'Till hell hath smoked it out!
But why hold out such secrecy o'er this?
   Mrs. Sto.   Be not impatient;
For I would have you wed this Josephine.
   Black.   Me wed the girl?
   Mrs. Sto. You wed the girl?—methinks a mighty honor—
   Black.   Aye, honor, yes; but if 'tis but for honor,
I never marry only for honor.
   Mrs. Sto.   But if I add a small-sized fortune to it?
   Black.   Aye, there you speak! my ear ope's wide his door
To let that sound come tripping gayly in!
   Mrs. Sto.   Hark, then, to me: If you will marry her,
And take her off to some far distant land
Where none will ever hear of her again,
Then you shall have a third of all her fortune.
Are you agreed?
   Black.   Am I agreed? Will you not give me more?
   Mrs. Sto.   Nothing.
   Black.   Then surely I'm agreed.
   Mrs. Sto.   Then so it is arranged.
   Black.   Nay, not so quick; am I to ne'er return,
With this sweet bride, to my own native land?
   Mrs. Sto.   Not with thy bride; but if she dies,
Of pestilence, or by the ague chill,
Or if, perchance, some reptile tastes her blood;
Or if some wild beast tears her limb from limb;—
Then you may come back to your native land!
   Black.   I'll not accept such terms as you have made.
   Mrs. Sto.   Did you not say you would accept my terms?
   Black.   Did I, i' faith, then will I change them now.
   Mrs. Sto.   For twenty years you've served me as a friend,—

Perhaps, at first, I did not think on this,—
Considering then, your many years of service,
I'll make your fortune half as great again.
    Black.   Now, like a Stoic, I must perforce accept.
    Mrs. Sto.   Then is our business over.   [*Exeunt.*

    Scene III.—A dining-room in Mrs. Stone's house in Berkeley.
                  Enter Servants.
    1st Serv't.   How long will't be before they have returned?
    2d Serv't.   From church?   About one hour.
    1st Serv't.   [*to servant girl.*]   You saw the marrying,
      Nell; how went it off?
    Nell.   How went it off?   It went off like a hearse
Over a precipice.
    2d Serv't. ·   I take you not :—
You know, good Nell, your wit does shine so bright
That ours is blinded by it.   Then tell us
How looked the bridegroom, and how looked the bride ?
    Nell.   I'll not tell that; I'll tell how looked the bride,
And then how looked the bridegroom.
    2d Serv't.   As you will.
    Nell.   Aye, as I will; then listen now to me :—
When all were gone I hurried to the church,
And, as I entered in, wild echoes rushed
From out their hiding places—then, like fiends
Cried out to one another !
Then came the minister,
And they stood up : the bride like a sweet lily,
On which black night doth scowl with her dark face—
And all the while the minister did read,
The dreary winds in deepest sorrow moaned;

Now loud and wildly moaning, 'till his voice
Was drowned: then, when they ceased, we heard his voice
   again.
   3d Serv't.   Last night I woke about the midnight hour,
To hear wings fluttering in the darkened air,
And then I heard the howl of dogs without,
Come riding down upon the fearful gale !
I have not dared to speak of this before,
But now I speak, since cause for it is found.
   1st Serv't.   And I was waked from out a horrid dream
By that same sound ;—then trembled all the house.
Against the window-panes each heavy blast
Led on the rain, and when the heavy gale
Dragged off a cloud, caught on the pointed moon,
By her dim light I saw, from cloud to cloud,
Strange white-faced spirits one another chase !
   Nell.   Ah, sadly do I fear me for this wedding !
                             [Roar of carriages.
But here they come !—then quickly to your posts !
                                  [Exeunt.

———

ACT II.

   SCENE I.—A room in Arden's cottage in the outskirts of San
Francisco.
                Enter JOSEPHINE and LILY.
   Lily.   Yes ; I am spending at my father's house
A few short days, the first in many months.
   Jos.   Now I am glad to see that face of thine,
That long hath been o'erspread with gloomy sadness,
Covered again with Summer sunned joy !
   Lily.   It is a mother's love, with smiles beginning

Watching the tender innocent young flower,
Just springing up to meet life's pelting storms;
Then does the mother take it to her breast
And guards it with a love that's greater far than death.
But tell me Josephine, is it then true
That you must leave for New York City soon?

Jos. Would it were not; alas, it is too true!

Lily. But you will soon return?

Jos. I think we will be gone about three months.

Lily. Goes Blackwell with you?

Jos. Yes; he will go;—I fear that man;
For he has got a smooth and oily tongue,
And eyes to freeze the blood.
His skin has, too, a sleek and oily look,
That is not seen upon an honest man.

Lily. And how is it your aunt has such a friend
In such a man?

Jos. That I know not;
Nor does her only son, your husband, know.

Lily. 'Tis strange!

Jos. Ay, strange it is; but, Lily, I have here
Some letters which my father gave to me,
That time he lay upon the bed of death,
Which he told me to open when I reached
My twentieth year. I ask that you will keep
Good charge of them 'till I return again.

Lily. Let not a thought in fear arise for them.

Enter MR. and MRS ARDEN.

Ard. And so you must so soon depart from us?
Would I could now bestow a fortune on you
Before you go; for you deserve it well;

Deny it not with those sweet maiden blushes,
They are the overflowings of a soul
More to be prized than all the gold of earth.
Since I have not a fortune to give thee,
Receive that which I have—an old man's blessing!
Though I would give it, if I had it now,
I will not wish your wealth were made of gold,
Which loved, destroys the beauty of maidenhood.
And could these shining things have tongues and speak,
'Tis my belief they'd tell more darkened tales
Of weary heart pains, guilty consciences,
Than deeds that we should pattern;
But I would have your breast free from those cares
That keep men waked o' nights;—that on the heart,
Do sit and brood, 'till but a nightmare's left—
And, with my blessing, do I say farewell!

Mrs. Ard. And let my blessing be aside of his!

Jos. Farewell! My fondest hope's to soon return again!

[Exit JOSEPHINE.

Mrs. Ard. How swiftly Time, upon unwearied wing,
Is ever fleeing back into the past;
The monster future slowly creeps on towards us,
While that poor sparrow, Time, affrighted flies
Into the Past, that prison cage, which, closed,
There's none so strong can ever open it.
It seems but yesterday that Lily, here,
Gave up her hand to her young, loving husband;
And then seemed Josephine but still a child,
That now is turned into a full-grown woman.

Ard. Life's but a breath, borne off by meanest winds;
Or word, that, writ upon the Ocean's shore,

The waves will wash away;
A fleeting thing, that sleeps and wakes and dies ;
A dream that is dreamed and is over !　　　　　*[Exeunt.*

Scene II.—A bedroom in a hotel in New York.　A door L. 2 E.,
through which enter Blackwell and Mrs. Stone.　A door R. C.,
which opens into a room behind the first.　R. 2 E., a window with
curtains hanging on either side.

Black.　Thy niece looks colder on me every hour !
Mrs. Sto.　Ha ! is it so ? and hath
Thy love not prospered ?
Black.　Prospered ?　I'd sooner woo the porcupine
Than woo thy niece ; for when I moved near her,
She shot her scornful glances,
As swift as flames from out a mitrailleuse,
And when I called here "rose," she called me "villain !"
Then, when I spoke of love, she said my tongue
Had stained that word, so that she ne'er again
Could hear it uttered, patiently !
I then sent out my thoughts o'er all creation
A-wandering, to gather pretty names,
Which, garnished with sweet accent, I did call her ;
But, all the while, she stamped with her small foot,
Nor would she lend attention to my speech.
Mrs. Sto.　And, like a craven, you gave up the fight !
Oh that I were a man but for an hour,
Then I'd make such a wooing for these maidens,
As they had never dreamed of heretofore.
Not with a mournful look would I gaze at them,
But with a glance that reached their very souls,
And they did tremble till their knees waged war
With one another !

For every soft and silly sigh they gave,
I'd give a curse, that so would frighten Love,
That, trembling, he would hide behind their tears !
But come, poor coward, at your work again ;
I'll be at hand to give you my protection,
If you are vanquished for a second time.
I'll go call Josephine, and bring her here,
That you may woo, and then I'll slip behind,
This hanging curtain, there to note your progress.   [*Exit.*

   Black.   Were I now one of these warm-hearted fools,
This Josephine I'd call a flower, and send up tears
To weep in my two eyes ; for she, unlike the oak,
Has no protection 'gainst the howling storms.
I'd harp upon her child-like innocence,
And then, perchance, some burning tears of mine
Would scald my feeble eyes.
But should I marry her, at first she'd weep,
And pale her face would grow ; but then we cannot
Forever look upon the blushing rose ;
At times 'tis best to see the cold-faced lily.

[Enter JOSEPHINE through door R. C., followed by MRS.
   STONE, who steps behind the window-curtain unperceived by her.]

But here she comes !

   Jos.   My aunt told me you had some weighty matter
To tell me.

   Black.   The matter is of such weight
My thought can hardly lift it unto you.
Oh now, my sweet, my bright-eyed Josephine--

   Jos.   Again this insolence !—and has my aunt

Given her consent to this—my degradation ?
It cannot be ! Ah, no, it cannot be !
 Black. Why, look on me, is it a degradation
That I have asked you for your hand-—your love ?
But this is but a mockery of anger
That's in your eyes ; a shadow of a frown
That's on your brow ; come let me take that hand
To see if anger trembles in it too !
 Jos. Stand off, you villain !
 Black. Now you grow cruel, lovely Josephine,
And in your eye a tear—a little tear—
It well becomes that pretty face of thine !
Thou'lt not say "no," that word would be my dooms-man !
 Jos. With all my strength I hurl then " No !" at you !
 Black. And I hurl " Yes !" for, be it known to you,
It is decided you shall be my wife !
 Jos. It is decided ? Who has made decision ?
 Black. Your aunt and I myself have done it.
 Jos. In her 'twas generous thus to give away
Another's hand !
 Black. Ay, it was generous,
And, for the gift, I thank her heartily !
I ne'er received so sweet a gift before.
There is a pleasing variation in
Your character : now 'tis all fire, and now
As calm as is a silent Summer's morn !
 Jos. But I will find a judge to guard me 'gainst—
 Mrs. Sto. [*entering from behind the curtain.*] I am
  your judge, and you shall marry him,
Or, by the heaven, we'll say that you're insane,
Or that he is your lawful husband now ;--

Jos.   And, ere I marry him, I'll find a judge
That is called Death, who cannot hear your tales !
              [*Springs to the door* L. 2 E. *and rushes out.*
Black.   [*starts after her.*]   I'll follow her !
Mrs. Sto.   [*holding him back.*]   No, still, be cool and
     think;—
She will return when leech-like hunger
Begins to suck her blood !
     Black.   But she may plunge into the bay's deep waters—
Mrs. Sto.   Then is the fortune made.
Black.   'Tis true ; then is fortune assured to us—
Mrs. Sto.   To us, say you? and is your mind gone wrong?
Black.   To us, I say ; did you not make agreement
With me, that I should have a sum denoted
If I should marry with this niece of yours ?
     Mrs. Sto.   Ay ! if you marry her.
Black.   And would you have me marry her dead body ?
Mrs. Sto.   If 'tis your pleasure to go marry her dead body,
Go marry it ; but I'll not pay you for it.
     Black.   Then, if she dies, you will not pay the sum ?
Mrs. Sto.   No !
Black.   Then I'll expose such deeds of yours as will
Make men's flesh creep !
     Mrs. Sto.   And I'll expose
A deed of yours—a morsel delicate
To feed a hungry halter on !—Have you
Been then so foolish as to think me so ?
     Black.   May curses on you fall from heaven like rain !
Mrs. Sto.   A fit one thou to call upon high Heaven !
But think not on her body being dead,
For, I predict that, ere a week be past,

Will she return, and then, by marrying her,
You shall obtain reward.   [*Exeunt.*

SCENE III—Time, night. A wharf at the end of a street in New
York. Snowing.

Enter JOSEPHINE.

Jos. Howl! howl! howl! ye chilly Winter winds!
Tear off this poor, weak flesh of mine!
And you,
Cold, cruel Winter, bring still your vast hordes on
Of snowflakes, armed with a shield of white,
That pierce me with their lance of chilliness :
Yet, even they have pity ; for, when they strike
Upon my cheek, they melt into soft tears.
Each hurrying cloud of Heaven grows black with anger,
To see me here ; a poor, weak thing,
That never wished them harm ! And, in
Each corner of these stony buildings, winds
Do howl and hiss at me. Oh, all the world
Has grown my enemy. How cold! how cold it is?
Three days ago—three icy, freezing days—
Was it three days? But I will see : it now
Is night, and then there was another night,
And then there were three cold, cold days,
When never a sun did deign to smile on me !
Three days? three days? and then two chilly nights—
No ; how was it?   [*Counts on her fingers.*
I fear my weary brain
Is hushed to sleep by this hard Winter's wind !
But now I'm free ! oh free ! free ! free ! But what is free ?
Tell me, ye pretty things—white-breasted snows,
And are you free ? Methinks, then, it is wrong

To let all things be free ;—there's one thing, though :
There is a tyrant governing in the world—
Whose name is Hunger.   Oh ! I'm hungry, and
So cold ! yet I will try to drag me on !

                                  [Gets up and moves on.
Perhaps there is humanity in the world yet—
[Stops surprised at finding herself at the end of the wharf.
And is this now the end ?
Where goest thou, thou deep and rushing tide ?
And canst thou lead me where there is no pain ?
No chilling snows, no cruel, stinging pains ?
What ! no answer here but stillness deep ?
Were I to take this leap, a muddy bottom
Would I deep down rest on.   And then I'd die,
And my poor, useless hands would sway about
To every motion of the silent water ;
And then the fish would come to gape down at
And see themselves in my wide, staring eyes.
And then, affrighted, would they dart away!
The moving tide would take me, inch by inch,
'Till all alone I rested in the ocean :
And there, perchance,
I'd lay me 'twixt two whitened skeletons
Of sailors dead long centuries ago ;
And there we'd lie, and rattle our dead bones
Until the judgment day.   Yet this is better
For men and Winter are cold.   I'll take the leap!
Enter L. U. E. CATHERINE, who creeps up and lays her hand
                      on her shoulder.
   Cath.   Nay, what is this? Have you a thousand lives,
To cast one off at every childish fancy?

Look up at me, my cheeks are sunk, like yours,
And hunger, too, has sunken in my eyes,
'Till they seem resting in two open tombs.
Come now with me; nay, think no more on death;
I'll pity you, and *I* will be your friend.
I have no food, nor kindly shelter for thee;
But, still, I have a heart, from which all warmth
Is not yet driven by this icy Winter!
Come, let your thoughts of death be banished!
   Jos.   Thou art an angel, sent from Heaven down
To save me from this rashness!
You spoke but now of hard misfortunes that
Had happened to you; tell them now to me,
That we may gently bear with one another.
   Cath.   You'd hear my tale? 'tis not a pretty tale,
Of how a lover woo'd, and prospered; but how, with cruelty,
He crushed the rose when broken from the stem!
I had a home once, like those you may see
When, hungrily, you wander Christmas nights,
From the cold streets, to see the happy faces
That past the windows flit with looks of joy.
That home is gone, for on a fated night
I did present this hand to one who ne'er
Laid aught of value on the gift I gave;
But ever grew to hate me more and more.
I know not why—I never did know why;
But oft I noticed when his face was turned
From me away, and bore a smile upon it,
That smile swift vanished if he looked towards me,
And angry hate sprang quickly to his eyes!
And then, at times, he'd strike me in the face,

And laugh to see the darkened spot come there!
One night he took me to a gloomy street,
And pierced me with his chilly-bladed dagger!
Nay;—but when he did think the breath was gone,
He called me back, and wept so piteously,
That though my mouth could not, my heart forgave him.
   Jos.   Forgive the man, that in his cruelty,—
   Cath.   Ay, for my love was such a love, that it
Did call a thousand small excuses up,
That plead for him, with words so filled with music
That they did calm my frowning soul, that judged
Until it gave the sentence of forgiveness!
   Jos.   And where is he, thy cruel husband, now?
   Cath.   My ear has grown a-weary, waiting long
To have some bird-like message light on it,
To whisper to me of his whereabouts.
O, I do fear that we will never, never meet again!
   Jos.   How strong is woman's love;—O, God, how freezing
Is grown this dark night's wind;—in listening to
Your sorrows, I had e'en forgot the wind.
                               [*Storm increases.*
   Cath.   I know a place that lends far better shelter
Than this one does; then come and let us thither;
We'll lie together, and may both keep warm.

ACT. III.

Scene I.—A valley back of Berkeley.

MRS. STONE discovered.

   Mrs. Sto.   A life of hate! the morn does lead in hate,
Until at night 'tis crushed off by sleep.

But I have tried to change this life of mine ;
And often I have wept.   Oh, how they'd laugh
To hear me say I'd wept.
But if they laugh, I have a laugh of mine,
And such a laugh as rings in tombs at night.
A strange queer world is this ; here all is war.
Here men, with eager eyes, strive on to get
The bread from others' mouths ;
Big animals do eat the smaller kind,
And men each other.   Then I'll sharpen up
These teeth of mine.—But here my poor fool comes.

Enter GODFREY.

God.   Oh, tell me quickly now of Josephine.

Mrs. Sto.   I fear that you will never see her more.

God.   What, never see her ?

Mrs. Sto.   Not in this world, but in that better world.

God.   But I will seek her.

Mrs. Sto.   Ah? and how will you?

God.   First will I ask of you, where has she gone ?

Mrs. Sto.   And I know not ; for, in an angry mood,
She parted from me.

God.   Oh, now have all the hardest strokes of life,
At one fell swoop come down upon my head.
Ah, now no more for me the morning breeze
Will play sweet music on the stringed sunbeams,
Nor lark sing out his sweet accomp'nyment ;
But only melancholy, hearse-like tunes.
No hope, say you, that I may find her yet?

Mrs. Sto.   Here does my son's wife walk at even-time,
Come here then in one hour, and ask of her :
For letters came to her from Josephine.

God.   Ten thousand thanks to thee, my dearest friend.
[*Exit* R.

Mrs. Sto.   A poor, poor fool.
Now for my son, with his suspicious mind :—
And I have poured suspicions in his ear,
Until such tumults raged within his breast,
That he was like a frothing madman,—
But here he comes, and much before the time.

Enter STONE.

Sto.   Who told you, mother, that they had met here ?
[MRS. STONE and her son hide behind a large rock, L.
Mrs. Sto.   My son, these eyes have seen it, gazed on it,
And sorrowed, Oh ! so deeply, at the sight.
Sto.   Often, say you, that they have met together ?
Mrs. Sto.   As oft as twilight blinds the eyes of day.
Sto.   Oh, God, what sorrows, mingle in with life.
But yesterday I loved a gentle wife
That then seemed pure, but now is stained as black
As hell with infamy !   But I'll not believe it !
You are not sure ? Oh, say you were not sure—
Say that—Was it not dark ?
Mrs. Sto.   Yes, it was dark ; but through that darkness
    pierced   .
These eyes as keenly as the new-waked sun.
Sto.   And then he clasped her hand ?
Mrs. Sto.   A saddest truth ; he then did clasp her hand.
Sto.   And did address her from his bended knees ?
Mrs. Sto.   And sued, and sighed, and called her "angel:"
Wept when she did, and smiled to see her smile.
Sto. . Then she was pleased to hear this villain's suit ?
Mrs. Sto.   She did not scorn it.

Sto.   Now, by the heavens!

Mrs. Sto.   Nay, wait and see these gentle lovers meet,
And hear them speak through sighs and lazy glances.
'Tis a sweet place to see them meet, my son.
From all the world, fairies here meet o'nights,
And hold their merry meetings.   Here Summer
So loves to dwell, that, when she needs must go,
She shrouds the sky around with clouds of crepe.
Here the best songsters, from earth's choir of birds,
Do flood the air with music—a lovely valley.

Sto.   It has no signs of loveliness for me,
But only bleak, high-rising mountain tops,
And sadness here is king.
Ha!

Enter LILY walking in meditation.

Lily.   Like some still stream, in which the oak-galls rest,
Her hate more bitter grows with every day;
And like a dagger moving in the dark,
Her words have meanings, that I see alone,
And I believe that this grandam, of late,
Would teach my boy to hate his mother, too.

Enter GODFREY, R.

God.   Oh, use, kind lady, now, that charity
Which all the world has long charged to your goodness—
I ask that thou wilt tell me where is she,
The gentle maiden that's called Josephine?

Lily.   Why, then, has some misfortune fallen her?

God.   Nay, seem not now as if you were astonished.

Lily.   But in pure truth it does astonish me;
I know of no mishap:—
Oh, tell me quickly who has injured her?

God.   I know of none; but tell me now which part
Of the round world is blessed with her sweet presence?
   Lily.   I know not.
   God.   [*Aside.*]   By heavens she carries it out well!
But I must urge more strongly.   [Kneels at LILY's feet.
   Sto.   Death!
   Mrs. Sto.   There's more to come.
   God.   Now do I cast me at your very feet,
And thus shall all my word be bended down
While they are pleading anxiously before you.
Oh, lady, hear, my love for her is strong
As is the knot which joins the day to night.
   Mrs. Sto.   His love must needs be strong—did you hear
      him?
   Sto.   Yes, I did hear him doom my life to devils!
But I will hence!
   Mrs. Sto.   Sweet son, be not so hasty—there's much to
      come.
Calmly await its coming.
   Sto.   Fool that I was, to take her to this breast,
When she, perchance, has oft lain on another's.
Oh, that the sun would now scorch out her eyes,
That lustfully looked love upon his face!
See how the wretch now gently smiles again!
Oh God! why am I thus so greatly cursed?
But I will hence; it pains these eyes of mine
To look upon her devilish guiltiness.
   Mrs. Sto.   Nay, stay, sweet son, and see the end of it.
   Sto.   I'd blind these eyes, dared they to look upon it.
                    [Exit STONE, followed by his mother.

Lily.   I swear to you, by yonder heaven above,
I know not where she is.

God. ˙ Then I have been deceived.

Lily.   Deceived ? no, I
Have not deceived you.

God.   But another has.

Lily.   And who, that other ?

God.   That I cannot tell you now ;
But I will find her, and I'll have revenge
Upon her foe.
For, if I am not wrong in my suspicions.
Some threat'ning cloud now hangs o'er Josephine.
Oh that I had quick lightnings for my coursers.
A chariot, whose wheels were wrought of thought,
To speed me quickly to my loved one's side.
Oh, that the stars which look on both of us
Could send me messages down on their rays
About my love —my Josephine.
Would while I slept, my thoughts would steal without
This brain of mine, and wander o'er the earth
In search of her.
And on the surface of a dream write of her.

Re-enter STONE.

Lily.   And have you come for me, my husband ?

Sto.   Aye, I have come.

God.   Good evening, sir.

Sto.   Good evening, sir.   I'll meet you at another time.
   Good night.

Lily.   Oh, why that brow so dark ?
Has aught of evil happened to you ?

Oh let me share your sorrow as your joy [Exit GODFREY.
They say a gentle wife can cure a pain.

Sto. Soft sounds to come from such a sepulcher—
Oh, would that now my swelling heart would burst!

Lily. Speak not, sweet husband, such hard words to me—
You never spoke so harshly heretofore.

Sto. Oh, what a wretch! so hardened, and so young.
A face, that takes the lily's whiteness on,
To hide a basest purpose.   Then she hath
Two eyes that mock the sky's blue innocence,
And yet they look from out a soul so dark.

Lily. Oh, cease your cruel words; if I've done wrong,
I'll drown that wrong in tears.

Sto. If you had tears, as many as the ocean,
'Twould ne'er be wept away.   Nay, come not near
Me in your guiltiness.

Lily.   And is it thus?
Oh Heaven, have mercy on me!
But I'm not guilty; Oh, I am not so,
Oh listen now to me; hear me, sweet husband,
Alas, I have no more than these two eyes
And this poor tongue to plead my innocence.

Sto. And they are false!

Lily. None, none to speak for me!
Oh that the winds had tongues, and silent night,
That creeps in every place; but all are dumb;
Dumb, dumb, dumb.

Sto. Ay, they are dumb, and hold their tongues in pity,
Lest, speaking, they would tell your guiltiness.

Lily. When I am lying on the bed of death,
Come to me, husband; then will you believe me.

Sto. Not even then ; but I'll not parley longer ; I'll be
   divorced ;
Would I were dead ; for I have seen your guilt.
And now depart, no longer stain my sight
With your cursed presence !
   Lily. And where then shall I go?
Into the night?
   Sto. Into the night. 'Tis well you have a night
To hide your shame.
   Lily. Kiss me, sweet husband, ere we part forever,
And if you pass my grave, when I am dead,
Know that the dead one there forgives you all.
   Sto. I'll never more pollute my lips on yours.
   Lily. Good-bye, my husband. Now my heart is broke.
                                        [*Exeunt.*

SCENE II.—Night-time. ARDEN and wife sitting at a table c. in
a room in their little cottage. A lounge R.
   Ard. Methinks, at last, that fortune's tide has ta'en
An upward turn.
   Mrs. Ard. I'll not believe it till that tide doth run
As swift as slides, far up the ocean's beach,
The thund'ring wave.
   Ard. Our Lily hath, as you do know, a husband
Gentle and kind ;
And fortune has, of late, glanced kindly on me—
   Mrs. Ard. Heard you aught, then?
   Ard. No,
   Mrs. Ard. Listen !
   Ard. I hear no sound.
   Mrs. Ard. Perhaps 'twas but a false imagination
That did deceive me.

Ard.   What was it?

Mrs. Ard.   I surely thought I heard a woman's wail,
Which half was hushed up by this sad night's wind.

Ard.   Oft doth imagination act truth's part
Even as an echo.

Mrs. Ard.   Hush!   [*Low wail heard.*

Ard.   Surely that was a woman's voice.

Mrs. Ard.   So I thought.

Ard.   Then I'll go out and see who it may be.

Mrs. Ard.   'Tis some poor beggar, perchance,
That mocks a groan to gain our charity.

Enter ARDEN with LILY leaning on his shoulder for support.

Lily.   Make up the little bed for me, Oh mother, now;
There let me die, for I am grown a-weary of this world.

        [ARDEN leads her to a lounge on which she lies down.

Mrs. Ard.   Why, what's the matter, Lily, what's the
        matter?

Ard.   Tell your old father, Lily; are you sick?

Lily   I'm sick of living—sick of living now!

Mrs. Ard.   But speak out and be plain.

Lily.   Hard thoughts of sadness crush my rising words.

Ard.   Has living being dared to hurt my child?
By Heaven, and if they have, I'll tear them limb from limb!

Lily.   Nay, father, ask the question not of me;
But let me die, and leave the bitter world;
For since that day, when I was born, it seems
That I have been the cause of strivings here—
Then let me quietly lay down to die,
And leave this world to peace.

Ard.   Nay Lily, let not your thought be overcome
By this down-heartedness—here is your mother,

That loves you, daughter, as none else can love,
Your father, too, and then your gentle child.
    Lily. I have no child! oh God, I have no child!
    Mrs. Ard. What! is he dead?
    Lily. For me, death's hands upon him.
Oh heaven, look pity down upon a poor,
Pained soul, and, with that glance, melt these hard bonds
That hold it here to earth; oh heaven! oh heaven! oh heaven!
And is it dark, my father? is it dark?
What are those bright things, shining in my face?—
Oh now I see, red glaring demons' eyes!
And is it dark?—oh now I do remember—
The stream of recollection, flowing back,
Will overcome me—oh 'twill crush me now—
Oh save me father, save me, save me, save me!—
See, there they come!
    Ard. I'm here, my darling child; what is it?
    Lily. Sweet beings tell me—tell me that again—
Like flower-spirits sleeping on a moonbeam,
Are your sweet whispers—no pain is there say you?
Sleep, sleep—hush mother, hear—what does—   [*sleeps.*
    Ard. Earth's harshest troubles have tormented her
Till reason was then spirited away,
But now she sleeps—in sleep let her be dead,
Until she wakens with renewed life—
Did she not say her child was dead to her?
    Mrs. Ard. My memory does tell me that she did.
    Ard. I cannot work its meaning out.
    Mrs. Ard. A dead child, yet he lives—and is he lost?
    Ard. Nay, that would not have raised this mighty tempest
In her poor mind.

Lily. (*dreaming.*) "Not even then."

Mrs. Ard.   Hush ! listen to her words.

Lily.   Where ?—but who goes by my grave—
You still will love me, Willie ?—divorced—

Ard.   Divorced ! then has he broke the law of mighty
    God ?—
I'm an old man, wife ; that ne'er did injure
A man or beast on earth ; and when God looks
Upon my memory,
Life's sweet recording Angel, he will find
That I ne'er tried to harm a butterfly.
Where in the sky, of this my heart, white clouds
Of love did only reign ; has anger come,
In darkened clouds, swift rising o'er th' horizon—
But ah, that anger is of no avail ;
What shall I do ? if I should take the law,
The law loves not to look on poverty,
And did I take the law in my own hands
These grey hairs would be called a murderer's.

Mrs. Ard.   His mother, though, hath kindness in her
    heart,—
She will wipe off the opinion that her son—
For some false reason—hath gained of our Lily.

Ard.   I love the woman not ; but it may be
That I do her injustice.

Mrs. Ard.   That you surely do !

Ard.   God only knows ; if I am wrong may he
With pity glance on one of those poor worms ;
Which he does deign to see, through worlds of stars ;
Apast the mighty sun, and past the moon,
Below the mountain tops, and by an ant-hill,

Crawling along, down in some new born wrinkle,
Upon this small earth's face,
   Lily. [*wakes.*] Where am I now? methought the night
     was round me,
And by a horrid dream, was I chased through it.
   Mrs. Ard. How feel you, Lily? and are you better now?
   Lily. Then all is true ! oh, that I'd slept for aye,
Then had it been naught but a child of sleep,
A thing so small, it ne'er could do me harm.
Better? yes, mother, I am better grown,
For there is a physician that is now
Fast healing all my pains—his name is death.
   Mrs. Ard. Speak not so, Lily, for you make me weep.
   Ard. Cheer up, my child, time yet hath garnered for us
Full many happy days in the near future :—
And what could we do, darling, without you !
   Lily. When I am gone do not grieve for me, father.
One that was ever in the way while here,
Will in a better dwelling be ; then grieve you not,—
And it may be, that while you sleep, your souls
Will leave their daytime home
To wander with me o'er the earth at midnight.
Now, father, lift me from this resting place,
And help me mother, to my little room.
To-morrow bring my Willie here to me,
To see his mother ere her soul has fled.
[*She leans one arm on her father's shoulder, and one on her*
   mother's, and so is helped out.]

   Scene III.—A room in Stone's house in Berkeley.
              Stone discovered.
   Sto. Oh, this anxiety does strain the nerves,

Until a breath might break them ;
Another to-morrow !   Then I'll to court,
And have this bond of marriage broke in twain.

Enter ARDEN.

Ard.   Young man, I've come to ask a favor of you—
Of you, my daughter's and my injurer,
But were she not now at the door of death
I'd never ask the smallest favor of you.
No ; not if thou didst own this breath of mine,
And, by the gift, could save me from black death.

   Sto.   She now is dying, say you ? no, she will not die.
   Ard.   How, sir, do you know that ?
   Sto.   Because I know whereof is her disease.
   Ard.   And I know, that 'tis from the hard effect
Of a long course of studied cruelty.

   Sto.   Nay, it has not been of a long duration.
With one hard blow it came, unto my knowledge ?
   Ard.   What came unto thy knowledge ?
   Sto.   Her guilt.
   Ard.   What, wretch !
[*raises his cane to strike, but drops it on second thought.*
[*aside.*]   But down wild anger !
For I must hold these passions well in check,
Or all her hope for happiness is ruined.
[*to him.*]   But, sir, I'll try to speak more calmly to you,
And, if my voice does tremble, lay't to age.
Long years have brought me troubles in this world.

   Sto.   Old man, I have a great respect for you ;
I know thou lov'st thy daughter, and 'tis well,
Perhaps, that thou shouldst never know the truth,
Did truth bring thee such sorrow as is mine.

Ard. I know how it is, as you, too, do know ;
You, who have ruined my poor, gentle child !
  Sto. An' you will have it that way, have it so.
Now tell me, what is that same favor, which
You spoke of ?
  Ard. It is no favor that I ask of you ;
It is that which I have a right to demand :—
My daughter's child.
  Sto. Your daughter's child is mine.
  Ard. It now belongs to both; ere long, it will
Belong to you alone.
  Sto. What would you with him ?
  Ard. I now would take him to his mother's breast,
For 'tis her wish to see him ere she dies.
  Sto. I grant her wish ; but this you too must know,
That when she does recover from her sickness,
The child remains not with her ;—by the law
He will belong to me.
  Ard. I know not that, for it does all depend
On circumstances of the case in hand.   [Exit ARDEN.
  Sto. Where am I now ? and is this place the earth ?
And are there stars, and is there night and day ?—
Or is it that from which we soon will wake ?
A fleeting, half-seen thing—dream ?   [*Exit.*

SCENE IV.—New York State. Open country, mountains surrounding.

  Enter CATHERINE and JOSEPHINE, who stop by a stream.
  Cath. Come, let us rest here on this mossy bank ;
This long day's walk has made my limbs grow weary.
  Jos. A pretty spot is this. Methinks that here

The busy bee must spend his holidays ;
The humming-bird, that drinks from flower-made cups ;
The ant, that does build up his mighty cities,
Come here to rest.   And then, perchance, they feast :
For tables having a white lily's leaf,
For napkins, white rose leaves, and for their plates
The golden buttercups.
  Cath.   A broken sunbeam for their knives and forks.
  Jos.   Aye, that was well ; and for their food, the bee
Would fetch his honey.
And when the dinner was removed, they'd have
A silver cloud, brought from the sky above,
To dance upon.
  Cath.   And for a sky, they'd have
A maiden dream of love, to hang o'erhead.
  Jos.   A pretty way is this to bid the hours
That are unwelcome, to depart from us.
This silver cloud you'd have them dance upon,
Brings back to mind the falling clouds of snow—
When first we met ;—thank God that I do now
Feel its cold chill but in imagination :—
Sweet Catherine, do you recall the hour ?
  Cath.   Ah, well do I, and two conflicting feelings,
Like night and day, do meet in memory :
The one—the bright one—tells me then I meet you,
The other, dark, does tell me of the storm.
And as the night is but a shadow of the day,
So is the suffering of that dreary hour
A shadow only to the joy of thee !
  Jos. Sweet friend, I thank you ; would that all my thanks
Did bear a thousand blessings on their backs :—

We have been friends in dark misfortune's hour—
Let us be friends forever.
    Cath.   Though we have
No other food, will live on that till death.
    Jos.   Last night I dreamed of those far off at home—
At home, said I?—I never had a home—
Of that far land, upon the Western shore,
Of which I told you.
    Cath.   Nay, you did not tell me,
Except that once you had a few friends there ;—
But tell me now, while we are resting here,
About those friends.
           Enter GODFREY and a DETECTIVE.
    Jos.   But who are these, that come with eagerness
Peering out through their eyes.   What ; can it be ?
    Cath.   Who ?
    God.   Now are you found at last, my heart's sweet
       treasure !
    Jos.   Found, found, found !
    God.   Ay found, my darling, after searching long
And wearily for you.
    Jos.   Now is the odor of life's flowers of joy
Borne to me by the breath of happiness.
Oh 'tis too sweet to be a thing of earth !
This happiness is far too sweet for earth,
Some envious thing will soon be creeping in
To murder it.
    God.   Oh that I had a pen, the which could write
The rose's breath, the drooping lily's hue ;
Then would I place, 'mid breath of flowers that die
Upon the lonely prairie, while awaiting

For the return of its long absent mate ;
Or birds that wept out songs of melody,
And in a prison died—the tales of these
Sweet moments.

 Jos. Now let me make known to you, Godfrey,
My only friend, except yourself, on earth.

 God. As you have been the friend of Josephine
I know that you are gentle, loving, kind,
And I do covet back the years now gone
In which I might have known you.

 Cath.   And all joy,
That you have felt at meeting have I shared,
And now may time, with each year, reap
A harvest of her greatest blessings for you—
Farewell!   [*starts to go.*

 Jos. Nay, but you shall not go !
You have
Been sister to me in adversity,
By your own wish ; and now, by my command,
You shall be sister in prosperity.

 God. There, Josephine did speak my thought for me.

 Jos. Then let us quickly to the sunset State.

 God. [*Aside to detective.*] And your reward shall be
 in a proportion
To this our joy.   [*Exeunt.*

 Scene V.—Same as Scene II, Act III.

Mrs. Arden discovered, R. Lily discovered lying on a bed, L

 Mrs. Ard. And are you better, Lilly ?

 Lily. Far better, mother.

 Mrs. Ard. Better, my child ?

Lily. Yes, mother, for the hour of death is gliding
Swift o'er my life as black clouds o'er the land.

Mrs. Ard. Oh, don't speak so despondingly, my child !

Lily. My spirits now are sunken deep down in
The prison of despair.

Mrs. Ard. Nay, think not so ; now have I news for thee,
'Twill make thy spirits like to sun-lit clouds
That move through Summer's sky.

Lily. What is it, mother ?

Mrs. Ard. Thy child is here.

Lily. Then God hath given an answer to my prayer.
Go call him, mother.   [Exit MRS. ARDEN.

Lily. Oh life, thou'st been a cruel master to me,
But I forgive thee for this latest boon.

Enter WILLIE.

Lily. Sweet boy, at last you've come to bless these eyes ;
Kiss me, my darling, kiss again poor mamma.

Will. What makes your face so white, my mamma ?

Lily. Sickness, Willie.

Will. But what has made you sick ?

Lily. Sorrow and pain.

Will. 'Twas a cruel pain to make your face so white ;—a
very cruel pain :—but 'twill away, will't not ?

Lily. Yes, Willie ; soon, soon now—
Do you remember, my boy. how, long ago, I told you of a
bright city beyond the clouds ?—beyond the little stars
you see peering through the dark at night ?

Will. Where the gold-winged angels are ?

Lily. Yes ; mamma will soon go there.

Will. And will you be an angel, too, and play sweet
music on a golden harp ?

Lily. I know not, Willie; but there will be the music of rest; for there is no more pain; no aching hearts, Willie.

The poor, poor soul, that's been weary here, does there find rest.

There the still river of peace flows ever on; no darkness enters there; they need no night to sleep; but all is day, ay, day forever there—

Oh happiness! and there is ever rest;

There rest the weary, and there the broken hearted.

No pain—no pain—no pa— — —   [*dies.*

    Will. Don't look that way, sweet mamma—oh now wake up—

Stare not so hard at me; wake. wake, wake!

Enter MRS. ARDEN.

    Mrs. Ard. Do you feel better now, my child?—What? —dead?

Oh now is all the beauty in the earth

A dead thing on my heart, a desert there;

Oh now are all the sorrows of the earth

In one great climax here!—Thou art not dead?

Oh say, with those white lips, thou are not dead!

Great Heaven, have pity on a poor, sad thing,

From whom rough death has torn her only child?

Enter ARDEN.

    Ard. Why do you weep?—Great God she is not dead—

Nay, Lily, thou'rt not dead?—speak to thy father—

Thy poor old father, Lily!—What, no words?—

Dead, dead, dead; 'tis cruel word! 'twill murder

All reason that is left! Forever gone!

Oh, Heaven in pity kill me; release me!

For now is all my life of nothing worth ;
Take it, ye winds, and blow it o'er the earth !
Dead ? say you ?   Nay, but that's too hard !   Change it :
Some gentler word put there.   Dead ?   Hush my child ;
Weep not so hard ; your mother only sleeps.

    Will.   And will she wake again ?

    Mrs. Ard.   Aye, angels in Heaven have already lifted
The sleep from off her eyes.

    Ard.   But sixty-five ? they say men live to seventy ;
And these, my years, have each borne on his back
His weight of sorrow ; but none like to this !—
Kind death release me, too !   Oh, how I loved her !
And in a moment—a poor piteous moment, —
It was all done !

    Mrs. Ard.   Grieve not so hard, good husband ;
The shadow black of death, while rounding earth,
Must sometimes fall on all ; — a lightning flash,
And then this life is swallowed up by death.

    Ard.   Then, sorrow, stand back, I will not grieve; I'll keep
You closed up in this heart until it burst.
Now I am calm.   Come, wife, I will, with you,
Prepare her burial.   [*Exeunt.*

ACT IV.

Scene I.—A room in ARDEN's cottage.

    Mrs. Stone discovered L.   Enter R. 2. E. a Minister.

    Min.   And the poor child's gone.

    Mrs. Sto.   Aye, gone !

    Min.   As gentle as the soft-breathed morning breeze.
But this great world, is a rough school indeed,

Where all are sent to learn.
Being wearried of her task.
The mighty master freed her, ere the rest.
Freed from the petty intrigues of the world,
Its harrassments, its cares and jealousies.
From strife for place; th' ingratitude of office;
From secret foes masked with the smiles of friendship
And hope deferred and hopes that are delusions;
From seeing honor jeered and vice triumphant.
The world's applause so many times misplaced,
Given to the self assured;
Its long forgetfulness of modest merit.
From the rich man's bloodless cold suspicion
That we would borrow whene'er we say good day.
The poor man's pride;
And from the anxious struggle on for bread,
The galling fate that makes us servitors
To some fat brained tyrannous accident
Who lords it well while in authority;
The tardy-coming justice of the world;
From seeing interest take the place of judgment
And blind the eyes of reason.
The birds ceased singing their sweet hymns of praise
To hear her voice.
Methinks the flowers will wear a robe of mourning
For this poor Lily dead.
And all men loved her.

 Mrs. Sto. I say, one did not.
 Min. I cannot believe it.
 Mrs. Sto. I know it well; a cruel, cursed wretch,
That ever sought to do her injury.

Min.   Nay, be not harsh ; this is no time for that ;
The sight should make us charitable.
Mrs. Sto.   Would'st be charitable to a devil ?
A very cursed devil !   Great God ! have mercy on me !
Min.   On thee ?
Mrs. Sto.   Aye, man ; on me !
Does not hell shine out through these eyes of mine ;
And in my heart can'st thou not see hot hell ?
Methinks 'twould make a very beacon flame
To light the world !   Oh, cursed, cursed wretch ?
Min.   Nay, calm thyself.
Mrs. Sto.   A dagger alone might calm me ! Oh, oh, oh!
I never thought that it would come to this !
And dead ? back, horrid word !
A poor thing, that never did me wrong,
And, in requital, I have caused her death—killed her !
Min.   What? you killed her ?
Mrs. Sto.   Not with a dagger, fool ;
But with a far worse instrument—'twas hate !
Min.   Perchance you do deceive yourself ; be calm ;
We all at times have said some bitter things.
Mrs. Sto.   Bitter! bitter !   Were all the clouds in heaven,
Of vapory, nut-gall juice, they'd be shame-faced
By this strong bitterness that mingled with my hate.
Min.   Speak not so loud.
Mrs. Sto.   Think you that she will hear, who's dead in
      there ?—
Min.   And if you hated her, what cause had you ?
Mrs. Sto.   Ay, that is right,
A demon whispered in my heart of hate.
Min.   Be not disturbed—'tis your imagination

That hath been worked on by your deepest sorrow :—
Lily did never speak a word of you but in a voice of kindness.

Mrs. Sto.   You knew her not, and I knew her to well;
She never did complain beneath my practice,
That gained success by using cruel arts,
But when I saw her lie so still and dead,
Her cold lips seemed so sadly to rebuke me—
Not harshly, as I oft had wounded her,
But with the voice of death so silently ;
Oh, then did memories swift flash on me
As the wild hurricane ; and each did have
For me a well-deserved curse in 's mouth.
Her poor, white cheek—and I made it so—
Oh, God, how then stood out each scene before me,
Where I had injured her, like fiends that torment ;
You are a man of God ; say, is there comfort
For murderers ?

Min.   Repent.

Mrs. Sto.   I have repented in hot flames of fire ;
For when I walk about, the echoes of
My footsteps scream out murderer ;
The breeze of heaven does steal up to my ear,
To leave their whispers ringing murderer !

Enter STONE.

Sto.   Long have I sought you, for I just have learned
That she is dead, whom once I loved so well.

Mrs. Sto.   And yet
Should have loved well, but that cursed jealousy
Did blind your silly eyes !

Sto.   Nay, but I saw.

Mrs. Sto. Saw her that was as pure as light of heaven,
Most foully wronged.

Sto. But did you not show me how that they met;
How his advances did she all accept;
How she rebuked not when he knelt to her,
But, with a smiling face accepted all;

Mrs. Sto. When he was asking her to tell him where
His Josephine had gone.

Sto. And was't that way?

Mrs. Sto. Ay, that it was.

Sto. And you did known it then?

Mrs. Sto. I did.

Sto. Accursed wretch! may heaven—

Min. Curse not! to God alone be punishment.

Sto. Oh it is hard, and then I was so cruel,
Heaping hard names upon her gentle head,
While she bore all, and said " I do forgive you."
And then, unlike a man, more like a fiend,
I sent her out into the chilly night.
So true a heart! and yet so injured.
Oh mother, mother, why have you done this?

Mrs. Sto. The answer that I once had given—is gone,
Her poor, dead face did drive it far from me.

Sto. You injure me, and cannot tell me why?
Bitter my life and murder all its joy!—
Stain a sweet angel with thy most foul words,
And cannot tell the why? oh 'tis too much!
Would I had died before I injured her;
Would had the lightnings torn my limbs apart,
And the great thunder crashed the heavens above
Till they did fall a shattered heap upon me.   [*Exit.*

Mrs. Sto.   And now I ask of you at what
Hour shall we bring her for the burial ?
 Min.   At ten o'clock, for in the following hour—
But no, 'tis needless !
 Mrs. Sto.   And then, perhaps, you'll say a few short
  prayers,
And sing a hymn ; a little weeping, and
Some earth thrown in ; and then 'twill all be over.
 Min.   All over here ; but I must leave thee, for I've
  work to do.   [*Exit.*
 Mrs. Sto.   And I will give you more, ere time be old.
There's mercy in a dagger's point, and I will taste it !
Or, better fate there may be found in drowning :—
Cold-blooded fishes, would you greet me then ?
Perhaps a shark would take me 'twixt his teeth,
And munch, and munch, and munch—a murderer !
                    [Enter BLACKWELL.]
And you too, here ? Come you death's courier
To tell the death of Josephine ?
 Black.   Dead ? no.
 Mrs. Sto.   Then I have naught to do with you.   Leave me !
 Black.   What ! is her mind estranged ?
I bring you joy.
 Mrs. Sto.   Joy lives not now ; it hath died long ago.
 Black.   To-morrow Josephine is to be married
 Mrs. Sto.   I know it well ; to-morrow Lily's buried.
At eleven, said he ? yes, truly, that he said.
 Black,   I said not that—good heaven, is Lily dead ?
 Mrs. Sto.   Dead ? Yes, she is dead.
 Black.   I know not of it.
 Mrs. Sto.   You might have known it for a year that's past.

Black.   Her mind is ill ; in truth a lunatic.
I ever thought her mind might come to this.   [*Exit.*
   Mrs. Sto.   A lunatic, ha ! ha !   I may be one.   [*Exit.*
                  Enter MR. and MRS. ARDEN.
   Ard.   How went the long night with you ?
   Mrs. Ard.   I could not sleep ;
My thoughts of Lily were so wide awake,
That from my staring eyes sleep fled affrighted.
At times I did half doze, and then I thought
I heard our Lily's spirit hovering near ;
And then I'd wake, and find myself a-listening,
But I could hear naught but the sound of stillness,
That in my ear did ring its dreary tone.
And then again I wept myself to sleep ;
And, in that sleep, I heard a voice speak to me,
And, as I listened, I knew that the voice
Was Lily's voice, as years ago I heard it.
The lilies came this morning.
   Ard.   Ay, that is right ; the white, white lilies,
Plucked from their stem of life like our own Lily ;
Lay them upon her.
   Mrs. Ard.   While I laid on the lilies, one by one,
I thought the heart that beat in me would break.
For she seemed sleeping, only that she breathed not,
And her poor eyes were gazing up to Heaven,
As if, with them she told life's sorrows there ;
And, oh, her cheek, so thin it was, and pale,
And her white lips were ope'd just wide enough
To let an unsaid prayer pass through.
   Ard.   Do you remember, wife, how kind she was,
Sharing all danger, that she might help those

Who were oppressed ; loving whom none else loved ;
Smiling on all with that sweet smile of hers,
Which taught us how the sunlight shone in heaven ?

[Exeunt.

SCENE II.—Inside of a church. GODFREY, JOSEPHINE, brides-
maids, etc., sitting in the front pew. A wedding march is played
on the organ, and the marriage party go forward and arrange themselves in front of the altar. Two sextons standing at a door inside
of the church L. 1. E. The minister enters at the vestry door L. C.,
and at the same time enter through the door L. 1. E. pall-beraers
carrying LILY's coffin. Not perceiving the marriage party, at first,
they walk about half way up the aisle, followed by the mourners.

Curtain falls.   End of Act IV.

ACT V.

SCENE 1.—A churchyard.   Time, evening.

Enter MRS. STONE, with her face heavily veiled.

Mrs. Sto.   I've grown a very baby since her death,
Kneeling and praying that perchance sometime
When does her spirit wing its way to earth,
'Twill have compassion on its murderer.
But to the world, that mimicry of hell,
I'll act my devil's part.   A poor fool I,
That when my mind was charged with distraction,
I rushed out to a meek-faced minister.
But time's returned me back my mask again;
The same cold brow, the cold as iron eye,
To stare a fiend out of his countenance.
Come down, sweet night, throw thy light garment o'er me,

[Kneels at LILY's grave.

For I would not that man should see me pray.

Enter BLACKWELL.

Black. And you a praying; ha! ha! ha!

Mrs. Sto. [*rising.*] Even here, too, are you then, fiend
of fate?

Black. Ambition hath not raised me up that high.

Mrs. Sto. Why do you, then, so follow me of late?
Were I to hide me in yon ghastly vault
Methinks you'd find me there.

Black. Ay, I would cast
The rotting bones at thee; and hollow skulls,
'Till echoes shrieked beneath each coffin lid.

Mrs. Sto. Have you no fear to speak thus in this place!
Here where pale ghosts do walk these nightly hours,
Wailing for sins once done upon upon this earth.

Enter CATHERINE, who hides unperceived behind a tombstone

Black. Come there a legion of white ghosts here now
I'd dare them all to pass this dagger's point.

Mrs. Sto. A dagger, ha! to murder dead men with?

Black. Dead corpses, no; but living ones, perhaps.
Nay, does your face turn white, your face? ha! ha!

Cath. Ha! ha!

Black. Did you hear that?

Mrs. Sto. 'Tis but a ghost, to dare your dagger's point.
But why flees all the blood from out your face?
Methinks 'tis white and milky as the moon.
Nay, call now back that sentinel of health,
The blood, into your cheek; thou art too bold.

Black. I do; I dare the fiercest fiend of hell!
'Twas but an echo. But no more of this.
I've followed you because

Of weighty purposes, that in the mind
Have wandered long, like your unresting spirits.

Mrs. Sto.   And what may be your weighty purposes ?
Tell them to me.   I long have been your partner
In secrecy; I'd be your partner still.

Black.   Then this is it : I would have from you
The fortune which you once did promise me.

Mrs. Sto.   Is this an hour to ask such things of me ?

Black.   I know not by what name you call the hour ;
But this I know, I love its look full well,
For in it does a fortune wait for me !
Or else there is a death that waits for you.

Mrs. Sto.   A death, say you ? nay, you cannot mean that !
You would not have these lips, that now speak to you,
Closed up for aye ?   Your only friend on earth,
The one that's known you for these twenty years,
To lie here weltering in the blood you spill ?

Black.   But, then, I will, if you have not the money
That patiently I've waited for so long.

Mrs. Sto.   Think well of it ; have my deeds been such
          to you
That you should pay in terms of enmity ?
And if I have not money, can my death
Have value as a payment when 'tis made
Think of the deed ; 'twill haunt you when you sleep ;
And while you wake, 'twill be a horrid shadow,
That conscience says all men do look upon.

Black.   Conscience, or fiends, or hell, or what you will :
If you have not the money, then you die.

Mrs. Sto.   If it must be, take this, my answer !
          [*Draws a dagger from her bosom and stabs him.*

Black. Curse you! you've killed me!

Cath. Murder! murder! murder!

Mrs. Sto. Ha! are the bloodhounds on my track so soon?
But I was never made to run from them.   [*Exit walking.*

Cath. [*Kneels down by Blackwell's side.*]   Met once
  again, but only met too late;
Alas! he's dead; but on his lips I'll lay
This cheek of mine; perhaps some lingering breath
Is hovering still where it has lived so long.

Black. Stand back, she-wolf! great heaven, art thou a
  spirit?
An airy mockery of my murdered wife?
But I will fear thee not, thou horrid sprite,
Though thou put on thy look of coldest horror;
Torment —

Cath. But I'm no spirit; I'm thy wife.

Black. So the dead lie, as well as do the living—

Cath. Oh waste not
That breath more precious than this life can tell:
Think quickly, for the time of thought is short;
And let each thought be bearer of belief.
I am your own, and still your loving wife.

Black. Your voice does have a natural ring.   But no.
With a cold-hearted dagger did I pierce
Her harmless breast.

Cath. Not from my body fled the breath away.

Black. How came you in this place, if you are a living
  being?

Cath. A providence
That shapes man's course on earth hath lead me to
This land.   To tell the why to you,

Would be to make a silly waste of time.
But this, in briefness, will I tell thy ear ;
To-day I saw you walking in the street,
And knew you well ; for long has memory
Kept watchful guard upon that face of thine.
And, when I saw you, at a distance, followed,
Trembling in fear of this my new-found joy ;
And, ere you stopped, the sun drew off the day,
And sent refreshed night to guard the earth..
When I came up I saw you speaking to
A women, that was half hid by the night ;
And then, because of fear to taste my joy
Too soon, I sat me down behind a tombstone.
    Black.   One sin, then, less to drag me down to hell.
    Cath.   Now will I ask that which, for long, long years,
I've hoped to ask, until the heart did grow
Hope-sick :
If it is true (which I cannot believe),
That you did have intent to murder me ?
    Black.   Nay, ask me not, for life is ebbing fast ;
But think that I did not intend to kill thee.
Oh, how hard pains chase swiftly through my body !
Ah, pain, thou are a music brought from hell !
    Cath.   Oh, would that I might bear you pain for you !
In sharing it the time would be recalled
When everything between us two was shared.
Then would come back those happiest hours of life,
When first I gave my love, my all, to thee.
Do'st thou remember how the morning breeze
Was telling the birds what pretty tales to sing,
And how they sang, and only sang of love ;

And how the brook did music play upon
The pebbles, that were ever rolling on ;
And how you laid your head upon my breast,
And said that you would love me then and ever ?
   Black.   Yes, I remember all ; but these harsh pains
Do make a target of my memory.
   Cath.   Alas, that I cannot a sharer be
In this thy pain, as then I shared thy love.
But lay thy head upon this breast of mine,
And then I'll weep a flood of chilly tears
To cool thy burning pain.   Now say to me,
And ease my anxious mind ere you depart,
You had not wished to kill me ?
   Black.   My life is short ; my breath is failing fast—
   Cath.   Oh, tell me quickly, then.
   Black.   I did !   Curse on
Thy woman's curiosity.   Oh, this has ended me !
                        [*Groans and dies.*
   Cath.   Gone, gone, gone, yet I will love you still ;
For once those arms did clasp me round with love ;
Those dead lips kiss me once—I love them yet.
And those poor eyes did look so lovingly.
Oh dead, dead, dead !

   Scene II.—A room in Godfrey's house. Mr. and Mrs. Arden,
Catherine, Josephine, and relatives assembled.

   Mrs. Ard.   We should beware in judging Josephine,
For, through mistake, I once did wrong poor Lily.
We think not when we have our loved ones round us,
And pain them with a bitter sneer or word,
That it may be before the hour of midnight,
Or, ere the sun be sunken down in darkness,

Their souls may pass out on that face of night,
Or, wing their way adown the sun's last ray ;
And then ?   The pale lips cannot answer then.

   Jos.   I do not seek to injure any one,
But hope to prove my aunt has done no wrong.
These letters, that I left in Lily's charge,
That, since her death, you have returned to me,
State, in my father's writing, that he left
A fortune for me with this aunt of mine,
Which on my twentieth year she was to give me ;
But she has never spoken to me of it,
And I know now that she is very poor ;
So here before her relatives I'd charge her
With keeping from me that which is my own.

               Enter GODFREY.

   God.   And did you hear the horrid news last night?
That friend of Lily's mother-in-law is murdered.
The man called Blackwell.

   Mrs. Ard.   Murdered ?   Who murdered him ?

   God.   'Tis only known a woman did the deed.

   Mrs. Ard.   How was that known, and yet the murderer
     not ?

   God.   A woman, once his wife long years ago,
Who had not seen him for these many years,
Saw him, and knew him, on the day he died ;
And, when she saw him, followed after him.
The time was evening, and beneath its shade
She saw him go in through a grave-yard gate ;
A woman there spoke to him for a time,
Then murdered him, and turned and fled away.

   Jos.   My husband, what have you heard of my aunt ?

God. Soon she will be here, and will tell you then.

Mrs Ard. And does she know why you have called her here ?

God. She does not know.

Enter MRS. STONE.

Mrs. Sto. This has resemblance to a merry meeting,
So bright the faces of this company ;
You should know, Josephine, such things I like not,
Then why have you made me partaker of it ?

God. I fear 'twill be as a sad merry making
As men do make upon a funeral.

Mrs. Sto. A funeral ? what ? but it cannot be.

Jos. Aye, but it is ; and sad the heart of mine,
That forces out the words, to tell it you.

Mrs. Sto. A funeral, but who is't now that's dead ?

Jos. My love for you.

Mrs. Sto. Your love for me ? ha ! ha ! and is it so ?
Then be it known I feed not on your love ;
And did I wear it for a garment on
This back of mine, I would not feel it there ;
Nor will it raise a fortune up to me—

Jos. It was lost through your guilt.

Mrs. Sto. Guilt ?

Jos. Nay, put no injured look upon your face ;
Your actions are stamped all with guiltiness,
Turn your eyes backward over twenty years ;
Canst thou see back, upon the plain of time,
A dying father and his orphan child ?
There canst thou picture, too, a guilty woman
Who robbed that orphan of its earthly all ?
Nay, hold not back ; lay out the truth before us.

Mrs. Sto,   And 'twas for this you trapped me to this place ?
To injure me with wrongful slanders ?
But think you I will meekly play the lamb ?
Make way there ; let me pass.

                             [tries to go out through a locked door

God.   The door is locked.

Mrs. Sto.   I'd crush the lock were it of adamant.

God.   Thy hand, methinks, is far too soft for that ;
But calm thyself ; here are you brought for judgment ;
These are thy judges that are seated here.

Mrs. Sto.   And can they bear the angry tigress' glance ?

God.   They will bear thine.

Mrs. Sto.   Nay, but this all is only some foolish jest ?

God.   Would that it were no more ; but, as I live—

Mrs. Sto.   But as you live—and all the life you have
Might by a tiny sparrow's brain be bounded—
Then judge ahead, and you, you moon-faced judges.
Put now a look of weighty wisdom on ;
Be wise in looks, if you be not in thought.
Keep your ears stretched to catch the slightest sound ;
Nay, never look amazed,
Now that I'm done, you may proceed to work.

God.   Then, be it known, full evidence is found,
That you have made what was once Josephine's—
A fortune left her by her father dead—
Your own ; and were you man, and not a woman,
You should be named a thief.

Mrs. Sto.   And were you man, and woman not, false liar,
I'd throttle you!--now judge, wax faces, judge !

Jos.   The time has not yet come for judgment on you.
Another tale 'gainst you I'm forced to tell ;

Long was it locked a secret in my breast,
'Till I did share that secret with my husband ;
Then, be it known to all this company,
That this, my aunt, who ever was so loving,
On a false plea, did take me from my home
To far New York, and there did strive to wed me—
   Mrs. Sto. Nay, you do draw all patience from my breast
By your slow speech. I'll tell your tale,
Then will the end come quickly. Grave judges :
My niece would say I wished to marry her
To some poor devil who would take her hand,
Being well paid for it ; and would take her where
She would be from my sight, while I here spent
The money that her father left her.
Now judge me daughter of the devil, or
A fiend, or what you will. But speak
A word to ease my ears, that itch to hear
A word from lips so grave.   [*Knocking at the door.*
   God. Who knocks ?
   [*Within*] *Police.* Two officers of law.
   Mrs. Sto. Ha ! stands it so ? The blessing of the devil
I leave to all of you ! Such friends, such piteous friends !
Curse all of you—like sparks of midnight fire
May curses fall on you !
The glistening gold and death are all man's earthly friends;
The last I love the best. Come kiss me, death !
     [*Draws a dagger from her bosom and stabs herself.*
Now on ! now on ! ye hounds, upon the dying hare !

FLAVIA.

FLAVIA.

A DRAMA.

ACT I.

Scene I.—Time, night. A room, through a window in which the Coliseum is seen, with the moonlight falling upon it.

FLAVIA—BASILIUS.

Flav. How calm and peaceful seems this hour of
    night ; —
See how the moon's soft rays come gently downward,
As if the watchful angels up in heaven
Had sent these cooler rays down from the sky
To rest so softly where the hot sun blazed,
That then the tumults of the angry day
Are soothed to silence.   The cries of pain are hushed ;
The soldiers' tread ; the rattling car of war
Break not the silence of the peaceful night;
The loud discordant jarrings of the day
Seem ever present where there is injustice;
But all the healing elements of the night
In silence work unseen.

   Bas.   'Tis but a respite;
To-morrow surely comes, and like a nightmare,

Takes on itself the dreary shape and visage
Of what was yesterday; and so each day
Has in it pictured forth scenes of oppression:
The hideous inequality of rights;
The self-same picture of a tyrant's power;
The merciless greed peculiar to mankind ;
And I to-morrow am driven to th' arena,
To fight with beasts, and murder other men.
I one time thought this world of ours was human,
But by the mass of wrong I see around me,
The cruel cowardice by which the strong o'ercome the weak,
I see that each man has within his nature
The passions of all beasts upon the earth;
I've seen the serpent coiled within his eye,
The fox, the tiger, and the murderous shark;—
I've seen them all in men.—
Such is humanity, with this exception,
There's something seldom used that's God-like,
To curb this world within him.
    Flav.   One time it would have made me weep to hear
      you ;
For then I lived where were the woods and plains.
I thought then all was kindness in the world,
For there the passing winds would kiss the flowers;
The flowers in turn would load the winds with sweetness;
The birds with gentle note would wake the morning;
And then the winds, that wandered through the trees,
Would murmur soft applause to their sweet music,
The while the smiling sun beamed down on all.
In memory now I see the rugged hut,
Close by the Danube, where my father dwelt.

I see my mother, with her soft blue eyes,
And all the people of that sweet old home
Seemed gentle—noble as the scenes around them,
Not harsh like grating Rome:—
'Tis like a vision now half past away,
For one day came the Romans to our land,
To burn our homes, enslave and murder us.
They brought my father, mother and myself with them:
But soon my mother pined away, and died ;
And since that time, a slave and gladiator,
My father fights with beasts, that gaping crowds
May laugh to see his danger.
    Bas.   True, Flavia, true; justice lives on the Danube.
Wherever men are found in largest numbers,
Man's greed makes jails and dungeons to be found.
His fellow-man he locks from light and air,
And treats him as no dog would treat another.
Where men in largest numbers come together,
They join together in vast bands for murder,
And shed more blood than all the beasts on earth.
And where the largest mass of men have joined,
Reigns most inharmony; nature is most defaced.
Here in this Rome
Murder is cradled ; here luxury and crime
Stare honesty swift out o' countenance.
Some laugh while others die; and some must die,
Because this reasoning being murders all justice.
Cowards in state sit in the Coliseum,
And that their leaden hours may be spurred onward
By ghastly scenes, have bold men murdered,
And watch them die, to start a Roman laugh.

Flav.   When first they brought my father here to Rome
He had a giant's strength ; but seeing blood
Come warm from human flesh, while the eye glazed,
Made him most sick at heart ; and often he,
While telling how a friend fell by his hand,
Has sighed most piteously to tell me of it ;
And often, were it not for me, he'd say,
He would have dropped his sword and shield, that he
Might fall in death, and end this barren life.
  Bas.   And still we cling to life through all our years,
As if this hell were heaven.   Since every day
Is made of disappointments, pain, and rebuffs,
It seems most strange that we should cling to it ;
In all the worlds naught can be found that's worse.
  Flav.   'Tis said that some one sought the life of Nero
While he went to the baths.   'Twas yesterday ;—
And is it true ?
  Bas.   'Tis true ; and all Rome trembles,
Fearing the tyrant's wrath ; for various classes
Have been suspected as the instigators.
And now the current of his suspicion
Flows strong towards us, and we are most suspected.
  Flav.   The gladiators ?
  Bas.   'Tis so ; for 'tis believed we wait but for the day,
And such a time as does invite,
To strike for freedom.
  Flav.   Why is't this way imagined ?
  Bas.   I know no reason.
  Flav.   Why was it that the one who sought his life
Was not then taken in the murderous act ?
  Bas.   Because unseen, and th' uncertain arrow

Came from a roof above.   Through all the day
The Emperor kept his palace, and all day
His spies have dogged our steps :
   Flav.   Oh, what uncertainty dwells in the air !
How I have longed that this uncertain life
Might have an end ; how hopelessly have hoped
This bloody panorama of each day
Might cease sometime to pass before my eyes ;
That yet a time might come when with each day
I would not fear the death of those I loved.
   Bas.   That time will come ;—
Aye, Flavia, that time is near at hand ;
For though some cowards still are found amongst us
Who, though they risk their lives each day 'gainst men or
      beasts,
Yet fear the merest whisper of this Nero ;
Still there are those with courage that knows no fear—
And with such men we'll cut our way to freedom.
   Flav.   And then, I know not how it is, I see a time,
Far, far away, and dimly in the future,
When all men will be free ; for in the past
I see that this has oft been so before.
For thoughts, like men, have died and risen again ;
And all the things our eyes can look upon
Have died but to be born a million times ;
And through the hoary ages of the past
There such a time I see repeated over
As oft as there are grains of sand upon
The edges of the sea.   I see that war
Has often left the earth ; pain and disease

And poverty have often fled from it.
And so they will when that time comes again.
    Bas. ıA pretty dream. With such sweet thoughts as these
The brain of man 's a heaven above the body
Where thoughts in starry constellations move,
And over them the spirit guides their way,
Leading the brightest upward.
    Flav. Why should it not come ? The universe is justice;
And when men learns to read the laws around him,
Should he not learn to cure his curious madness ?
When he has learned to read that deeper language
That has no words—which gods speak each to each ;
When from the dasies, the lilies of the field,
He learns to speak a language made of wisdom,
He'll learn the laws by which men should be governed ;
And from the teachings of the smallest flower
Learn what in justice all our laws should be.
Learn that the winds go equally to all,
The rain on all falls equally alike,
The sunlight on them all does fall the same;
What each takes from the earth, that is his own :
To take from out the earth its sustenance
Each has a right—so the air's denizens
And all the savage beasts ; but men are mad
And have forgotten these sweet rules of justice.
But when they take their laws from out the earth,
As they now get their very life from it,
Then will the age of peace come back to them.
The earth from pole to pole is but a book
Whose marvelous tales are written by the light
Upon it's thousand pages ; its words are perfumed

By sweetest essence from the rose's breath ;
Its letters colored by the violet's hue,
While diamonds cast their light upon its pages.
The midnight stars have read it in the dark ;
And all the winds of heaven learn there their music ;
And all the beings of the universe
Read there for truth. But man, being dull of learning,
Has never read aright,
And got the chords of nature out of tune.
But when this lyre of heaven plays sweet again
Mountains will change to air,
The earth become a vapor, and all things
Float softly on the music of God's love
Back to the realm of justice.

Bas. Ah ! Flavia, 'twere well to still dream on,
And with such fancies kill reality.

Flav. Although my father now lies sick abed
From his most cruel wounds, and though I have
Sat by him through the hours of all the day,
He has not spoke to me of this uprising,
Nor have I heard from any one but you
A whisper of it.

Bas. The secret is well kept. Though we are feared,
No floating rumor has passed from us
To tell how we have joined ourselves with others
And of our deed. And when our hope is reached,
Oh, Flavia, then we begin to live,
And I again call myself a man.

Flav. Oh, happy time !

Bas. For me, even then, the sunlight of that time
Would all be lost by overshadowing clouds,

And all my thoughts be like the sun's bright rays
When murdered in that darkness
If Flavia would not become my bride.
Oh, Flavia! again I ask your hand,
And for that boon for life I am your slave.

    Flav. How many men desirous to be slaves
Have turned their slavery to tyranny!

    Bas. I would be tyrant, then, to all my acts,
Until they lived to serve you.

    Flav. But—

    Bas. Nay, speak not yet, but hear me to the end ;
For though your words to you may be as light
As the light breath that lifts them, they have power
To shatter all my life.
For since the time when first I saw your face
My thoughts of you have stood out to the front,
And have since then held sway o'er all my others,
And have built up my fondest hopes in me.
To crush these hopes were like to blot the stars
From out the night
And leave black midnight reigning in my mind.

    Flav. I cannot love you now; for all my love
Is gone, beyond recall, out to another.

    Bas. Oh! call those words back to the mouth that spoke
        them ;
For now they seek an entrance to my brain
To murder all my peace. Hear me, sweet Flavia!
How can you be so cold! Why, all my life
Stands trembling on the threshold of this hour
To wait your judgment.

Oh ! if you were but mine, how I would live,
My only end to make your hours grow bright !
   Flav. My love is like the past—beyond all power
To call it back. It pains me much, indeed,
To speak these words, if they have wounded you.
   Bas. Wounded ! The end of this is worse than wounds :
Your words, like funeral flowers, will deck the grave
Of hopes all dead. My life from this time forth
Grows but a barren waste ;
A lifeless desert, stretched out to where the sun
Sinks into night. Oh, Flavia ! how I loved you !
And then to end in this—in nothing ;
And now those pictures that my fancies wove
Fade like the leering, mocking shapes of midnight !
Oh, speak one gentle word !
Send it as a sweet medicine to soothe
My tortured mind. Is there no place for hope ?
   Flav. What shall I say ? What is there left to say ?
My only answer can be but what I've made—
I have no other.
   Bas. Then farewell, Flavia ; now I go forth ;
My years in youth grown old; for all the world
Bears to these eyes the shriveled look of Winter,
And all my hopes fall downward to the earth
Like the white snowflakes of that bitter time.
                            [Exit BASILIUS.
   Flav. Oh, what a world is this !—most tyrannous.
A world that makes us cruel when we would be kind,
Without a wish, or any favoring desire,
But 'gainst my wish, and quite against my will,
I have been forced

To speak those words which build up disappoinment
Most bitter.   Yet the while is in my bosom
Pity most deep.   What is it I have done?
Re-enter BASILIUS,

  Bas.   Nay, speak no more; the bitterness is past.
I have been most unmanly in complaining;
'Twas but a moment; again I am a man;
And as a man, from that point am your friend;
And that great honor you've conferred on him,
That you make master to control your love
Binds him to me in closest bonds of friendship;
One look, sweet Flavia, and I am gone.   *[Exit.*
  Flav.   Oh, but this sight to me is piteous,
To see him, with all his mighty strength,
Bowed down with grief.   And yet indeed 'twas sweet
To hear such words of love; but then such love
Makes pity more; 'tis true his love was true;
But when he spoke of friendship—his love being hopeless,
I saw that in his eye which makes me fear;
Something that spoke of future enmity;
And yet 'twas pitiful; most pitiable—
How sad the orbs of heaven seem to mine eyes!
Methinks they look most sadly on the world,
Noting how all things end in sorrow here;
Why, 'tis enough to make the heavens look sad,
And all the twinkliug wanderers of the night
Keep on their way in silence ;
And yet he bore himself most like a man,
Uttered most noble sentiments of this,
Our state.   Talked of our present servitude,

And with a soldier's tongue did talk of freedom;—
Yet still I fear him.

Enter GOTHARVA.

Goth. Flavia!
She hears me not. Her mind is dwelling on
Some gentle deed, some kindly charity;
Some act which will accord
With that kind look which dwells upon her face.
Flavia!

Flav. Oh, Gotharva!

Goth. Sighing, sweet one! 'Tis not your wont to sigh;
That gloomy brow looks not like Flavia.
But often have I seen a sparkling laughter
Dance in those eyes, like sunbeams in a stream;
While peals of merriment, a most sweet music,
Sprang from your lips. What, tears?

Flav. No woman ever yet heard that I've heard,
Saw that which I have seen, and did not weep.

Goth. Has some one dared——

Flav. Because the fault was mine, therefore I wept;
Ask me no further.

Goth. If it would give you pain I'd ask for nothing,
Were't even my life.

Flav. O, kind Gotharva! 'Tis thus you ever speak.

Goth. Because I have no power to speak but in that way,
When I speak of you.

Flav. Oh, sweet, sweet words!
To hear them makes me dread the coming future
Lest they should change.

Goth. Flavia, they could not change;

For in those eyes a more than magic spell
Holds me against all change.
 Flav. But still I fear; let me not think of it;
For when that time has come, then I would die.
There is a dread within me now of such a time:
This cruel fear came to me first to-night.
For as I gazed upon the vault of heaven,
The stars seemed trembling ; and vague images
Of hideous shapes, gazed at me through the dark ;
Hush ! Who was't that spoke ?
 Goth. Fear not, sweet one ; 'twas nothing !
 Flav. See there ! A face !
        [GOTHARVA goes and returns.
 Goth. 'Twas but a picture painted on the air,
Drawn by your fears.
 Flav. My mind is filled with a most cruel dread ,
Should we be parted, think you when we are dead,
There is a world where we will meet again ?
 Goth. One time I thought that all would end with death,
For then I'd read but man's imperfect nature ;
But when I saw in you how God made woman,
I knew there was a world beyond the stars ;
That all this gentleness, all this perfection,
Was never doomed to die.
 Flav. It seems but just
That when this weary life of hopes unanswered,
This most delusive dream of passing shadows,
This weary and tumultuous life were ended,
A world of peace would come
Where all the jarring acts and sounds of life
Would never enter.

'Twere most unjust that we should turn to dust
Like the inanimate rock, that never knew a sorrow.
    Goth.   Most sweetly reasoned.
    Flav.   And there will be no change ; then you will love
    me
Through all the time to come.
    Goth.   As I do now ;—then will we still love on
Until the myriad years have flooded the future,
And yonder glittering lamps that light the heavens
Burn dim, and all the hoary-headed years
Pass halting by.
    Flav.   And now good night.   While such thoughts dwell
    within me
Let me now seek for sleep, that that sweet angel
May whisper in my dreams again,
And yet again, those words that I have heard.
    Goth.   Good night, my love.   Good night.
               [They go out, after which BASILIUS enters.
    Bas.   Oh Fate ! thou'rt cruel to some : but most to them
In holding me to listen to their words ;
For every word they spoke but added to
The deep revenge I'll take.   Am I not injured ?
The mightiest wrong a woman does a man
Is when she loves another.   So shall my vengeance
Be mightiest in my power !
It is a rule of time that I have seen,
That all things we desire will come to us ;
If we are most intent to have them and will wait,
Why I will wait and then will wait,
And still will wait, until I've murdered all
The happiest hopes they have, and thinking me

The dearest friend of all they have on earth,
Their every act shall lead them on to ruin !
Sweet Flavia !   Most gentle Flavia !
How easy 'twas to spurn my worthless love !
I, that was made to head all other men,
You rate so low.   But one day you shall bleed !

———

ACT II.

Scene I.—Laarchus and other gladiators in a room in Laarchus'
house.   The doors and windows, which are heavy, are barred.
Laarchus, who is sick, is resting in a chair.

Laar.   I feel, yes know, that ere the hours are late
I'll reach that milepost on the path of time
Where death, with visage grim, awaits my coming ;
And that the world, with all its many scenes,
Its jealousies, its petty strifes and hatred,
Will, like a passing scene, fade from my eyes.
Hence, have I called you here
That we may take this remnant of my life
To study out the road that leads to freedom.
Would that these walls, this place,
Were safer than it is; for as I've learned
The keen eyes of our foes, like stars of fate,
With evil portents shine upon our acts.
But as it is my wounds have held me fast ;
Therefore those words that I have harvested,
If they be said at all, must be said now.
And first of all let me unload myself
Of that which in my heart of all stands foremost—·
Of Flavia.   [*Flavia sobs.*

My child, weep not.   There is no cause for this.
Have I not told you
Death's but the evening hour of rest, when all the stars
And all the glories of an unseen world
Come out to greet th' enraptured wanderer.
When I was but a child, then like a child
I feared the foolish dark; that as youth
Tumultuous fear gave place to lesser storms;
That in the calmer, bolder hours of manhood
I scorned such childish fear; for at that time
I saw naught in this dark to make me fear.
When in full blooded youth, my careless eyes
Saw in this gilded, tinsel show of life
What made me love to live—and loving life
Is all that makes this childish fear of death.
But now I'm old, I've learned that in this death
Is but one of full many longer sleeps,
With dreams that pass beyond these earthly limits.
And those who've learned t' interpret that sweet language
Wrote by the sunbeam on the wild rose leaf,
Scrawled by the wintry blast on mountain tops,
Or bellowed by the loud resounding thunder,
Will learn to laugh because they have feared death
As children fear the dark.
For you, dear Flavia, I leave you what is more
Than wealth or jewels—these, my oft-proved friends;
And when I ask them—as my last request
To stand your friend, they'll turn to warriors
In your behalf.
  Gladiators.   Ay, that we will !
  Goth.   Let never a fear for her disturb your thoughts.

While in this arm is strength and life to move it,
Myself and all my life lives in the thought
To be of service to her.

 Bas. In that quick speech you first have seized the words
I'd use to tell how by your side I'll stand
Through all my life, still her protector.

 Goth. 'Tis spoken as I know you, and as my friend.

 Laar. Oh, gentlemen, those words come to my heart;
They overcome all else, and crowd away
The words I'd use to thank you. Hear them, my daughter,
And let the pride to know you have such friends
Assuage all grief. Here, in this box, my child,
You'll find some things that were your mother's once;
And when I'm gone, take them and make them yours;
Besides, you'll find in this some words of counsel;
The fruit grown from a life of many years.
Study them, Flavia, as I have done,
In getting them for you.

 Flav. Oh! my dear father, I shall study them,
Not once, but yet a thousand times again,
Till each particular word charms back to life
Some memory of yourself.

 Laar. And then, my child,
(While I wish not to chain you to that course,)
In some small points you'll find wrote there my wishes
How you should act.

 Flav. 'Twill be my dearest purpose
To make those words the fate that leads my life.

 Laar. Go now, my child, and leave us to this matter
That's yet before us.   [Exit FLAVIA.
I have heard late rumors

That Nero, his mind filled by his fear with madness,
Has the thought fixed most certain in his mind
That he who sought his life was one of us.

    Byrsa. Such is report; and fixing fast this rumor
Comes now the order of the Emperor
That either he who sought to take his life
Or else some other of our company
Be given up to die for this offense.

    Laar. What reason's given for this unjust suspicion?

    Byrsa. None.

    Laar. Aye! so; 'twas ever so. For have we yet
Seen reason given, or justice done by him?
Oh, if the evil deeds of those that do them
Must still be seen by them, when they are gone
Wandering and circling through this world of ours
By most fixed laws, creating inharmony,
And they must hear it, throughout all time to come,
Listening from out a world of harmony;
How will he suffer!
But in this lack of reason on his part
Stands now the stronger reason for your action.
I long have cherished the thought, ever sweet,
To be your leader in this crowning act;
For still is in these veins a soldier's blood,
And still my thoughts, that never a tyrant touched,
Did urge me to that end. But 'tis too late,
For in an hour or two, or ere the night,
I'll pass beyond this earth where slaves are made
Free from the slavery of the poor to the rich;
Of weaker to the strong; of dust to dust.
    Yet though I am not here, still there are others;

In some that blood, tinged but by unchecked nature,
Which in their cheeks had wrote eternal shame,
If they'd become less free than heaven's winds;
Has any action
Amongst you yet been taken, to choose a leader?
   Byrsa. We had a meeting in the Catacombs,
And by the vote we took we choose Gotharva.
   Laar. That was well done; you could have made no
     better.
Come close to me; my eyes are growing dim;
My time draws close at hand; yet one word more—
When th' all important moment comes, let courage
Fill every heart. Beware a moment's fear,
For fear so often takes the look of guilt,
The foe will feel that right must be with them,
And come against you with redoubled fury.
Fear 's at the bottom of all earthly woe
And does invite all those who would oppress;
Gives a temptation to a thousand wrongs;
While dauntless courage bears a charmed life
Against all dangers. My eyes are growing dark.
Courage, my friends! I see with other eyes
A grander time that's moving towards the earth.
Sages will laugh to hear it; and then fools,
Using their natural language, will deny,
But still it comes! The heavens push it on;
A million movements of the earth sing of it;
Far in the future I see the glorious day
When peace will reign again upon the earth.
The colored lights that made our atmospheres
Have faded one by one; the grander light,

Which is the sum, and more than that of all ;
That melts all pain, shines on the world within us,
Which shows that love and wisdom both are one ;—
The earth is moving onward towards that light
To glide beneath its flood of soothing rays,—
As beauteous as the snowflakes ; even now
Its broken rays begin to fall on earth
In each good deed that's done.

 Byrsa. Dead !

 Others. Dead !

 Goth. Our strongest fortress fallen ? Here was a mind
That towered above us all ?
The first time ever I saw his face it pleased me,
Marking what he has been at all times since.
Why, now he's dead,
Full many counsels sage that he has uttered,
Scarce heeded proofs of all his nobleness,
Come crowding in to tell me what he was ;
And yet I've often marked this thing in him—
He seemed unconscious of the truths he spoke.
But now he's gone ; the gates of speech are barred ;
The doors of hearing closed against the world ;
And even the sun's ray could not pass those eyes
To watch where he is gone.
Ah ! but we all shall come to this at last !
Here on this border line shall all grow equal.
Infants we come to earth ; till middle age
Brings out the things within us ; then we die;
Till in old age infants become again,
And pass beyond. But then some nobler minds
Move upward on the circle ere they die,

Into that life which most men find hereafter ;—
And he was one.
    Byrsa.   Why, now he's gone,
I see his nature as I never saw it ;
And now recall his many noble counsels.
I most remember what he said one night,
While the sun sank in clouds of fire and gold.
He chid me then for quarreling with my fate,
Showing that to the wise wisdom is in all things ;
That as each thought touched our remotest parts,
Changing our bodies, so opinions change ;
That those who suffer most, but take swift strides,
To find a mightier compensation for it ;
For all things in the universe are balanced.
That men on earth,
In those relations which they bear to each,
Are moved by laws as fixed as those same laws
Which sway the planets and the stars of night ;
That each man had a power to perform,
Some act no other man on earth could do ;
For each man has his own superior part
That all the road to heaven lead there through silence,
And by as many paths as there are men.
That as the tides were lifted by the moon
So was the tide of life in each raised up
By a sweet power that ruled the acts of men ;
And then he gave a thousand mighty proofs
That showed to me a life beyond this one,
Beyond all doubt.
    Goth.   It seems as if a well-fixed law of nature
Hides all the greatness of the noblest minds

Until they are no more; but then the thoughts passed
    through them
Must live though spoken not, while petty minds
Sport in the sunlight of the passing time.
          [Enter FLAVIA.]
    [*She falls on the body of her father and weeps.*

SCENE II.

BASILIUS.

Bas. A hypocrite; yet who could prove it in me?
'Twould take a giant to throw me off my guard;
I've play'd the virtuous man so long a time,
My inward self should make my outward form;
A soft and easy-going gentleman
That moves on tiptoe through this rugged world,
And by a smile makes other men his friends,
And so moves to his end. Ah, but 'tis sweet
To smile on those we hate—and I have some,
Because their kindness passed beyond endurance,—
And by that smile to make them slaves to us.
Ah! How th' unseen superior powers around us,
If such there be, must smile to see our acts!
How they must laugh to see these would-be gods
Blown up by their conceit;
Frowning like Jove upon a world of worms!
Now this Gotharva has a noble bearing;
His eyes placed on the line that makes perfection,
The latest round found in the ladder of nature;
No stormy brow to mark an angry mind,
Nor nothing likened to a chopping sea,
Not the dead level of a barren waste;

There's nothing oblique and nothing treacherous,
But all is harmony,
And therefore Flavia loves him and loves me not ;
Yet over all this greatness will I reach,
And, smiling to the end, make Flavia mine.
                    [Enter GOTHARVA.]
Good day, Gotharva ; what news ?
'Tis odd ; the moment ere you entered, my thoughts
Were on you.
I warrant you were thinking evil of me.

   Goth. You ask for news ? You ask a heavy load
From off my shoulders.

   Bas. How so ?

   Goth. Why, in this ; that my best friend, as I thought,
Has proved to be my bitterest enemy.
It seems most bitter that these many years
My warmest love has been all cast away
Upon a barren soil.

   Bas. 'Tis truly so ; and I have known such times,
When learning those I'd ever called my friends,
Had trampled on the love which I had given,
It shook my faith in man,
And all the world seemed jarred and out of tune ;
And then being thus disturbed, a bitterness
Would work an entrance like a deadly vapor
Murdering my peace.

   Goth. And that which made this sudden coming know-
     ledge
Seem harsher still was in the news it brought,
This long-loved friend seems not my foe alone,
But proves a foe

To all my plans, to my most cherished wishes;
And worse; for he that I had thought
Possessed all the highest attributes
Proves even a coward, working in the dark;—
To gain his murderous ends, lies through his smiles;
Speaks sweetly to us, with murder underneath;
Most bitter news, for mark me closely,
A traitor is amongst us!
   Bas. I had so feared.
   Goth. And mark this, too, ev'n if he was my brother,
Aye, did my mother's blood course through his veins,
I'd be the first to run a dagger through him.
'Tis one thing
To act the open foe; and in that case
The rules of war would lead a soldier's mind
To give the very brutes their benefit;
But to the secret method of the serpent
There is no rule but death. Mark me again;
The one who falters when the time has come,
Or dares to act the traitor,
Should hope for nothing!
   Bas. This is most true, most excellent,
And to my mind. But why this tone? These words
Would seem to bear with them something besides
That which you speak.
   Goth. Why, this, indeed, is strange—this innocence
With which you come upon the meaning of it;
And yet I thought it was no mighty matter
For one so skilled in all the cause of it
To see my meaning.
   Bas. Now, as you are my friend, withdraw those words—

But no, I will be gentler in my tone—
Yet to withdraw them were kindness to yourself ;
For now I see it all ; an enemy
Has whispered in your ear some slanderous tale,
Growing from out his own malicious nature,
Or founded else upon unjust reports ;
And then have you, (justly suspicions in our noble cause,)
Grown colder in your friendship ; at those foul words
Forgot that through these many years gone by—
But no, I will not speak—since you mistrust me
I have no heart to speak in my defense ;—
But yet I'll say you do me wrong in this,
For if you have forgot your love for me,
Mine is of stronger stuff, and not that kind
Which starts with credulous ears at every tale.
Have you not called me bold full many a time ?
'Tis cowardice that makes us weak in friendship.
Has not my friendship stood through many a year,
Oft in the face of death,
Offering my life a shield 'twixt you and danger—
Was it not so ?   Perhaps this is my fancy,
For now my mind is grown disturbed indeed.
Yet once you were my friend ; therefore for that
Let me forgive this wrong, though from this on
We grow most bitter in our enmity.
   Goth.   This is most true ; that you have many a time
Endangered ev'n your life to save my own.
   Bas.   Now that you say 'twas so
I see that it was most unkind in me
In such a way to be a traitor to you ;
Let me forget such baseness.

Goth. It was the highest act a friend could do.

Bas. Mention it not ; consider these things undone :
For my part I am willing to forget them,
Seeing 'twould show my hatred was not honest;
For in my foe I'd think of naught that's good.

Goth. (*aside*) Either I've wronged him, or there's in
doing right
Some power and quality that's so divine
That the mere shadowy semblance of itself,
Serves ev'n for villains as their mightiest weapon.

Bas. And if I stood with all my life, most willing
To offer it a sacrifice for yours ;
What thing is there esteemed of greater value
Than my own life, to prove me traitor,
Since I have offered that to prove my friendship?
If there is consequential logic in these acts
To prove me base, lower than man's degree,
Why, then I am the man for open war.
You'll find me then as steady to that end
As I was once in friendship.

Goth. Were you not seen to enter, late at night,
The Emperor's gardens ?

Bas. I was ; and I saw those who watched me,

Goth. Why did you go ?

Bas. I rather would be called a traitor still
Than tell you why.

Goth. Then I demand it from you.

Bas. Since you demand, I suppose you must have it,—
To place before the Emperor the proof
That he who sought his life was not yourself.
I did not wish to speak of this unkindness,

But you have forced me.   Now, lest again
My words be doubted, I shall bring the proof,
And fetch up witnesses to prove that true
Which I have spoken.
   Goth.   It shall not be,   [*seizes his arm.*
Oh, how our suspicions lead us to rashness.
Forgive me if you can ; forgive this rashness.
'Tis I who have been false beyond forgiveness
To one who proves indeed my truest friend !
The weight of my unkindness hangs upon me
Heavier than lead.
   Bas.   In justice to myself I would bring proofs,
So you may know that what I've said is true,
Nor doubt me more ; for as I was your friend
I'm willing now to bolster up my statements
With evidence to show I am not false.
   Goth.   Oh, speak no more !   And let me now atone
For my injustice, by, from this henceforth,
Stopping my ears against the slightest breath
That blows against you.
Let me add interest now in acting right
By way of payment for the wrongs I've done.
Having such proofs before of your great friendship,
How I believed you false I cannot tell, -
Unless that doubts admitted to the mind
Breed by the million, and by their disquiet
Make us grow mad.
   Bas.   But lest your mind should change its present state,
(For men will change their minds, and that most queerly,)
It is but just that I should furnish proof
That I am honest.

Goth. It shall not be. Myself I'll not dishonor
Another time by making such a contrast
Between your noble deeds and my own baseness.

    Bas. [*aside*] Oh, excellent stubbornness! For without
      this
I might have fared less well.
You would have had all my forgiveness
In such a cause if you had still condemned me;
For in this matter every act of caution
(Ay, if its vigilance must touch our friends)
Deserves our highest praise, and to condemn it
Were base in any one.

    Goth. Most nobly spoken,
And yet this nobleness of yours
Reproves me more.

    Bas. 'Twas not yourself;
'Twas that unjust suspicion that did speak,
Wrought by th' insidious whisperings of another.
The more I've seen the more this truth appears,
That we should not condemn the acts of others,
But pity only; therefore did I pity,
For 'twas no act of yours, but your misfortune.
I knew your mind, that justice steered its course;
Your mind was built upon a nobler plan
Than to condemn me. No, it was that madness
That enters us when slander drugs our reason.
But let these thoughts be buried to rise no more.—
What news of Flavia?

    Goth. Why, she seems better, though her father's death
Bears hard upon hear.

Bas. But then the words of counsel he has left her
Must serve somewhat to comfort her sad hours?
Goth. She has not seen them yet, fearing to see
The last of that which was so dear to her.
Bas. There speaks the woman's nature. She keeps
   them
I doubt not, ever close beside her.
Goth. Yes. In the room I've seen her stand for hours
Gazing upon the casket with sad looks;
And then she'd go and touch it with her hands,
Thinking, perchance, to raise sometime the lid,
And then would shake her head and walk away,
Leaving it still unopened.
Bas. Still womanlike in this. Poor Flavia!
Goth. Oh, it was pitiful! But now good-bye.
There is a matter that must call me hence.   [*Exit.*
Bas. Unsuspicious, forgiving, daring, generous!
And for these traits so easy is to lead
To his own ruin. I have seen rougher work.
Now, had he but been skilled in the ways o' the world,
I had not got so free from his suspicion;
But now he lies disarmed of all his weapons.
He's but a plaything, to spurn whene'er I wish.
Poor fool! This weakness of a generous nature
Would make him stand my friend against all proof,
Thinking he wronged me once.
And then, sweet Flavia, though you are odd,
One touch upon the spring of vanity
Opens your woman's nature and shows all.
And now my well laid scheme is ripe for action,
I'll have that casket; write in that same hand

Her father used, as his most solemn request,
That Flavia shall unite herself to me,
And that as his last dying request
She shall not speak of this to any one.
Why, I will act the part ev'n of a dead man.
Enjoining on his daughter his last wish,
And from the tomb call to my bride that will be.

ACT III.

SCENE I.

BASILIUS—DEMETRIAS.

Bas. Demetrias, what is't you wish?

Dem. It may seem odd—but nothing.
I've come to bring you news.

Bas. 'Tis nothing new. Of that commodity
There's but an ounce in twenty centuries ;
And our wiseacres but repeat to us
The stale remarks of dead men.

Dem. 'Tis nothing new, and yet 'tis something old
Which you know not.

Bas. It stirs the bile that's in me
To hear men talk of genius—their inspirations!
They're but compilers ; thieves from old books,
Acting upon the principle that to all men,
But those who're in the secret, things are most strange.
They rob us of the offspring of our minds—
Eternal repetition's nature's law—
Yet slowly reaching upward, adding to it.
'Tis an odd world of contradictions, this.

Demetrias. Why, I have often laughed to see
Scoundrels call others scoundrels for those acts

They itched to do themselves ;
And our receptive opposites condemning others
While deeply envying their cruel misfortune.
The folly of mankind oft sickens me :
The lies of history that call those great
Who 're pigmies atop the roaring waves of nature,
Riding in terror till there's calm again,
Then boasting her deeds their own;
Then for the mightiest men the world has known
The laws of nature governing the time
Use them as dusty pipes through which to speak.
    Dem.   The slime of ocean, from which we first emerged,
Still clings to us : and like the growths of ocean
We're most unstable in our movements,
The creatures of a million accidents,
Against our wills moved by a million laws,
Coming, we know not whence, without our wills,
And whirled against our wills we know not whither :
And we are to ourselves
The greatest puzzles of this odd creation ;
The penalty for solving it being death,
We spend our lives seeking its solution.
    Bas.   Yet man is vain !
And in his vanity he calls the wisdom
Found in the lower orders of creation —
Because the bee outstrips him
In architecture, the bird in music ; because
The smallest insect here is more courageous.
'Tis instinct ! Instinct ! It is my belief
That there are grains invisible in rocks of granite
Moving and circling as the bodies of heaven ;

That there are nations of beings upon each one
Governed by laws as perfect as are man's.
Man is the rust through which this world of ours
Is wearing away ; his spirit a careless word
Spoken by this world to some world beyond—
But fodder in the monstrous jaws of death
To be digested to some other state.

 Dem. I see philosophy has got her hold upon you :
'Twere best to leave her.

 Bas. When the sun stops then will we cease to think.
What is it you would tell me ?

 Dem. That yesterday—

 Bas. Tell me the future—that cornucopia
Filled with the solid prizes yet to grow
Upon our oddest fancies of to-day.

 Dem. I saw Lucillus ; told him our plans were laid
To take the traitors, and he left me then
To see the Emperor and tell him of it.

 Bas. Demetrias.

 Dem. Well ?

 Bas. You'll find that Flavia has a certain casket,
In which are kept concealed some writings
Wrote by her father in his latest hours.

 Dem. I have seen it.

 Bas. She keeps it in her room.
Here is a writing ; if you could place this in it
Without her knowledge, unseen by any one,
And keep this secret covered by the dark
That hides the inmost recess of your heart,
Why, that same act would bind me to your service

For all my life to come.   I would myself attend this,
But that the strongest reasons urge me 'gainst it.
    Dem.   Flavia goes to-day
(Following her usual custom) to weep again
Over the grave wherein her father lies.
While she is gone. I'll do it.

SCENE II.

BASILIUS—CLAUDIUS.

Bas.   You must see the Emperor about this matter.
Being so near to him, and trusted by him in so many
points, you should be able to induce him to grant more
time in which to perfect my plans.

Claud.   I have spoken to him ; but it is dangerous to
repeat the matter, for he is subject to sudden and violent
anger, which takes all reason from him.   But for the
friendship I bear you, which led me still to urge delay upon
him, the ringleaders would have been converted into
peaceful corpses long ere this.   But I promised that you
would furnish proof against all who had been engaged in
the conspiracy, and urged that in the present state of Rome
it were best not to act without some show of proof with
which to deceive the people.   To this he assented, and
said that he had noticed that strong governments were
maintained chiefly through the practice of deceiving the
governed ; and then he said that he would wait until they
could be deceived on this point.   He says that he mistrusts
you much, for he has a strong antipathy to red-headed
men ; and he has heard also that you are a bastard.   There
must, therefore, be no more delay, for he changes his deter-
mination with every new passion that springs to his mind.

You have told me that they meet again to-night. They must be taken at that time.

Bas. Since it must be so, why, so it must. You know where the body of our old friend Scylla lies buried in the Catacombs? I doubt not that when a boy you have often played hide-and-seek in the neighboring tombs.

Claud. I have; and the hair of my youthful head has often sprung up in alarm when some companion came creeping through the dark passage-ways behind me.

Bas. Turning to the right when you have passed his grave, you will find, if you have a light with you, a heavy slab leaning against the wall, which looks as if it had not been moved for ages. Upon opening it you will find what resembles a miniature temple, in which my friends meet to-night. Let your men be there at midnight, for by that hour they all will have gathered there; but do not have them there before that time, for my friends will come to the place one by one, according to previous agreement.

Claud. Now, for these services so valuable to the Emperor you must name your reward.

Bas. Oh, that I were a citizen of Rome, that I might make a fitting reply! I would then use my holiday words to say that I scorned a reward for patriotic services; and for these noble sentiments I would reap the applause of my countrymen, and they would elect me to some public office which had annexed to it the power to tax them, blood-suck them, and sell my honor high! Alas! that I, being born equal with other men, and coming here a pauper like the rest, should have become entangled so soon in the customs made by those who went before me, while

others are permitted to travel the smooth highway of life!
No, in common language, I will take no reward.

Claud.   Fear not to make the sum too large, for the
Emperor values your services most highly.

Bas.   I fear his gold might soil my spotless hands :
Wealth makes us cowards, for loving it.
It grows next to our life, a part of us,
And being a part of us, the fear to lose it
Does make us timid in each thing we do,
And makes us fear both friends and foes alike.
No, I would still be poor and charitable,
And having naught to lose, outface the devil.
Like all truly good men, I would find my reward in my
own just acts; for through all ages, history tells us, the
noblest patriots have ever expressed a profound disgust
when gold was offered for their services.   But, like a
drunken man, I am speaking of trifles as matters of im-
portance.   Good acts come from the inward unseen ray
launched by angels through the sunbeam, whose light alone
can reach the soul within us.

Claud.   You're proved a man of honor by your words.

Bas.   And yet words should not be trusted.   I thank
you, though, for this sweet, sweet flattery ; it is most dear
to me.

Claud.   And yet before in all this life of mine I never
knew a noble act but came from base desires, if we would
but be honest with ourselves, and dare to acknowledge it.

Bas.   Claudius, we're lice upon the back of earth ;
A most disreputable set indeed ;
Therefore we should be sanctimonious.
The hog has reached a high development in us ;

The vulture and the cormorant nest in us ;
By our fierce greed we 'mpoverish those who're weak,
Tramp down the sick, the halt and blind,
And when our puffed up skins are filled with blood
Death pricks us.

Claud. Then why not receive a reward for your services ?
If 'tis revenge you seek, the receipt besides of gold will
never mar your purpose ; and if love prompts you, if you
were as hideous as the Gorgon, you could buy it where you
would ; and as women are surely at the bottom of all our
earthly acts, you had better get it. If you seek fame, it is
sold in all quantities in the market to the exclusive few
who have the money to purchase it, and it is better to buy
it than to wait until after you are dead to have it.

Bas. I were a child if I did not see the profundity of
your thought ; but it were best to avoid wisdom, as a
friend of mine was kind enough to inform me ; for the
more we get of it the more melancholy we grow, and our
friends who are not affected by the disease might take us
for lunatics, which would be a pity. I would rather be a
lively ass than to make the profound discovery that all is
vanity, and be a wise man.

Claud. You will be at the place of meeting ?

Bas. Is my presence so essential that it cannot be done
without it ?

Claud. It might be done, but there's no cause for fear.

Bas. There are times for each thing ; and many times
When nature's laws, seizing those things we do,
Will drag them to success against all odds.
As this is of them, there 's no need for me.
Besides it is unpleasant to kill one's friends.—

Do not attribute this in me to fear :
I learned this long ago—
When danger is opposed, its hideous form
Shrinks from our view and fades away to nothing.
But there are matters of sentiment in this
Which holds me back.

    Claud.　So be it then.　We'll find them
By your directions.　　　　　　　　　[Exit BASILIUS.
There's villiany !　But they who deal in wrong
Ever make this mistake : to underate
Those they would play upon.　In their schemes
There's still some trifling matter left unnoted
Ev'n by the shrewdest, which siding with justice
Will yet defeat their ends ; and in this case
He sees in me the servant of the Emperor
Most trusted by him.　Yet if I'm not wrong
I see the signs of Nero's overthrow.
The soldiers of the legion in the North
Are in that wavering state when feathers change them.
The outlook is rebellion.　In the East
I mark the self-same sign.　Th' oppressed of Rome,
The slaves and gladiators, if they rise,
Will find success and victory for their efforts :
Why, then like other men I'll imitate
To find the safest road ;
And in this world of traitors I'll be one ;
But first I'll learn the secrets of Basilius,
Of which I have a glimmering, and I'll use them
To my best ends.

SCENE III.

FLAVIA—DIANA.

Diana. And still I hear your sorrows make wintry
    weather ;
That with each day you still weep o'er your loss.
There is a proper time for every grief,
But when it is prolonged, it grows a judgment
Which doth condemn the act and will of heaven.
    Flav. 'Tis not in me to raise my feeble thought against
    the high and mighty will of heaven,
Since I am but a dot ; my time is nothing
Where worlds have lived and died to mark the moments
And mighty systems swept the far beyond,
And lived and died, and died and lived again,
To mark the seconds in the hours of God.
'Tis not an impious mind that makes me sad,
And if it were the being I humbly dream of
Is so far up beyond condemning us
For our poor thoughts there is no measure for it.
But I being human
Still think upon my father's words of guidance,
His gentleness and his unwavering kindness
And weep that this is ended.
    Diana. But, Flavia, you should make this your comfort,
Your father's life was one prepared for death.
We should not weep when good men die, but rather
Bid them God-speed to leave this world of woe.
We've not yet lived while in this womb of earth,
But when we are delivered, then we live.
Then, when the good are born, why should we weep,
Since they are nobly built for some new world,

To learn the wonders of it.
When loved ones die, we have the reason still
To grieve a year from now, as grieve to-day.
    Flav. 'Tis not the icy reason.   There's something else
That grieves when we have lost the ones we love.
    Diana.   But may not those who have departed from us
Grow sad to see our sorrow?
    Flav.   It may be so,   ·
And I will strive to tear from out my mind
The bitter, yet sweet, memories of the past.—
But no, I cannot, for it seems each thing
My sight falls on at once grows eloquent
Of all that's lost,
    Diana.   Then to the truths of this, fancy adds more,
False in its essence.
    Flav.   Who knows 'tis false?
I have suspected that imagination,
Ev'n in its wildest flights, still looks in truth,
That in imagination
We see disjointed parts of things to be.
The reason why I have not ope'd this casket
Is that these vague imaginings of mine
Have made me dread some fearful secret in it.
    Diana.   Presentiments turn true to cowards;
But courage o'ercomes them all,
And for that reason
The sooner it is opened then the sooner
Can you prepare your mind to leave this sorrow.
Besides, sweet Flavia, it seems to me
That this does argue that you lack respect
Touching your father's wishes.   Why,

'Tis like a child to be so timid.
You dream too much.   Though you believe them
Dreams are the sportive children of the dark,
Grown in the brain, when closed up, shrunken, deformed,
Lacking that sunlight which is the food of thought.
  Flav.   But I've known other dreams, and in these dreams
My eyes grew keen ; and to my poor five senses
A thousand new etherial ones were added,
Which now are being developed in mankind ;
And through a light as white as driven snow,
I saw the secrets of the world :
I saw the human race had all moved westward,
Crossing the seas, rounding the globe a thousand times and
        more ;
I saw the object of mankind on earth
Was to discover their next resting place,
That till they'd found each secret of the earth
They would not find that higher realm beyond,
But love could lead them to it.
I saw a force that swept and eddied o'er this world of ours,
As the winds move, creating waves of thought.
I saw my former self seeing a thousand things,
Yet seeing not ; feeling a thousand things
That swept against me as they eddied onward,
Yet knowing not.   As in the realms of nature,
So in the undiscovered country of man's thought
I saw a latent power
To quell the anger of the lightning's flash,
To soothe the hurricane ;
I saw men groping in the dark for that
Which they saw in the light, and yet saw not,

And in these dreams I've seen that all is life,
And that this life moves all of nature round us.
But what I'd known as death was no more death,
But only one of many a longer sleep
To follow after many a day of life,
Till all the secrets of the earth are learned.
And death and ignorance at last were left;
As age would follow age in all the past,
I saw new rays of light grow to the sun;
And by the hues within the lights of heaven
I measured all their ages; :
I saw things now to us invisible
Dwelling within a different form of light,
And saw a form of light by which this earth
Is made invisible to other senses.
And then in dreams I've gone from star to star,
And on I went, treading the paths of space,
And saw the many worlds where we must dwell
And must subdue, and by a centripetal force
Make all their knowledge grow a part of us.
And then I saw the worlds that were asleep,
And others waking from their midnight dreams.
Then everywhere I saw that human love
Was the same force that dragged the planets onward.
    Diana. Why, what a fancy dwells within your mind!
    Flav. All truths are fancies when we hear them first--
First laughed at, then denied--at last believed.
    Diana. And will we all then reach this realm of fancy?
    Flav. All in their time,
For heaven's love forgives and draws us upward.
The mighty universe is linked in chains,

And the signs of the times are the strongest signs
Of the times in the future,
And angels above us drag us onward still.
Have you not seen that thoughts, theories, societies, governments ; things animate, and called inanimate ; earths and
suns, the worlds above us, pass through the same paths and
stages ; are built on the same plan and by the same laws ;
begin and end alike ? Yet every hour lifts them still upward, the tide being on the flood.

Diana. Why, yes, it seems as though it might be so.

Flav. All thoughts, all acts, all worlds,
Are on the homeward march ;
Their roads being backward on the beams of light ;
Those rays once so diverged their light was lost
Dimly begin to shine.

Diana. Now, Flavia, I must leave you,
But strive to rid yourself of gloominess,
And to that end go out among your friends ;
Walk often in the sun ;
See things whose shining pictures in the mind
Will leave no place for gloomy ones to hang,
And when you can, then come and visit me.

Flav. Farewell, sweet friend. [Exit DIANA.
And is it true ? Has she correctly chidden me in this ?
Do I, like some, make goblins of every passion ?
And does my sluggish nature, held back by fear,
Prove disrespectful to my father's wishes [*She goes
 to a casket and takes out some trinkets and a writing.*

(Reads) "*My Dearest Child—While you read these
words the hand that wrote them is mouldering in dust;
and yet, even when I am gone, it is my wish that these*

*words which I have left behind me shall be for your good.
I have studied the thoughts and acts of those who were our
friends with most exact care; and knowing that in the
stormy days to come some one should be your close protector I have selected as most worthy of your choice one
against whom no slur can be cast, no slander spoken.   Having justice and honesty in him, he is without fear.   I have
seen him proved noble in his attributes a thousand times.
Knowing that it would be to your own great good if you
were to marry him, if he should ask your hand my dying
wish is that you will not refuse this request from Basilius.
Speak not of this to any one.   Your Loving Father."*

What ?   My father ? are these his words to me ?
Oh, that these words had power to end my life !
And yet it seems not like him.
Yet here's his words.   I'll show it to Gotharva—
No ; that, too, is forbidden.
How heavy is my fate !   Yet I must bear it
Nor murmur at my lot, for he was ever
My only friend—a thousand times my friend ;
And then my father.   Oh, but yet 'tis hard ;
But in this wish must be some hidden purpose ;
And knowing him so just, must trust him here.
But, oh, how hard !   'Tis more than I can bear.
Must I give up the one I love so well,
When all my woman's nature is founded on love,
Which is the fountain head of all our deeds,
And am denied to tell him how I loved ?
If I could die, 'twere not to disobey ;
Would I were dead—at rest within the grave.

ACT IV.

SCENE 1.

DIANA—NURSE.

Diana. You say that Flavia is still abed, kept there by some strange sickness, of whose cause the doctors give no account?

Nurse. In all my days I have never seen its like and it is many the sick bed I have watched since I was young; but none like this. Oh, it was pitiful indeed, most sad, to see the poor child in such a state of mind; for she will not hear you till you speak to her many times over again, and then it would make your heart ache to hear her. The doctors shake their heads gravely when by themselves; call her sickness by strange names, and when with her, feel her pulse often, look long in her face, question her, but can do nothing to help her.

Diana. And can do much by such looks to make her worse. More than one patient that might have lived have been murdered by the long-drawn countenances about their beds.

Nurse. And what is worse, 'tis my belief they know nothing about her trouble.

Diana. Does she sleep well?

Nurse. No; that's the worst of it, too; and during the long nights she lies like a monument of marble, with her eyes staring wide, and as rigid as in death; and they never move, except at times, when a shudder passes over her, and then she looks with staring eyes to see I know not what; after which she moans most pitiably, but will not speak. Sometimes I ask the darling what she sees. She only shakes her head from side to side, moves her lips as if she were swallowing, sighs, and still says nothing.

Diana. Let some one go to her who knows how to make her laugh ; for there's more medicine in a laugh than in a whole apothecary's shop. How long is't now that she has lain abed ?

Nurse. ´Why, let me see. It was Tuesday my brother came. The day before was Monday ; yes, Monday. I came on Satnrday, and three days before were to be added to that, and this makes nine in all. The strange thing is that she told me this morning that she would get up to-day, for Gotharva was coming, and she must speak to him, as perhaps it would be the last time. *Laws a-mercy, child!* says I, *you must not. No indeedy. It would be the death of you.* She looked me straight in the face a moment, and then says she : *Would it were so Martha;* for she always called me by my first name ever since I used to sing her to sleep in my arms when she was a child. The young people in my day never got into such a way over a little love matter ; but times have changed, times have changed ! Then she called me again. *What, honey love ?* said I. *When I'm dead, nurse,* said she, *take these trinkets and these locks of hair and these letters,* says she, *and take good care of them, for they were dear to me.* When she got up she seemed as strong as ever, only she was pale. I asked her what she was going to do, and she replied, as if she were talking in a dream, that she would obey her father's wishes, even if she must die for it. They talk about men being stubborn, but women are stubborn, and will have their way. *Tut! tut! tut!* said I, *sweet one, don't take on so;* and the tears came to my eyes, for I couldn't help it. She has dressed

herself all in white, and is sitting in her room.　Ah me!
what a mighty tempest a little love can stir up.

Diana.　Did Gotharva know of her sickness?

Nurse.　No; for he has been away.

Enter FLAVIA.

Flav.　I hear his step.　He soon will be here now.

Diana.　What, Flavia?　Do you not know me?

Flav.　Know you?　Could I so soon forget a friend.

Enter GOTHARVA.

Goth.　Your face is pale; Flavia, you have been sick?

Flav.　But now seem well.　Indeed, am almost well.

Diana.　She needs more chiding for her fearful fancy,
Which seems to be a cure to all her life,
Then medicine to cure her of her trouble.

Goth.　What seems like fear in her is something more.

Diana.　Well, if it is not fear, 'tis melancholy,
And you should scold her for this gloominess;
For when not checked it will take root in us
And gain a stubborn hold upon our natures,
Yet sweet and hard to part with.
Therefore, I'll leave you, for I know you'll chide her,
And cannot bear to hear your cruel words.

Goth.　Would that I had the power by my chiding
To drive away this paleness from her cheek,
And then, by gentle words, to woo again
The bloom back to her face.

Diana.　Try, then, your magic;
It may be that, unknown to you, you have it.

Goth.　It may be so.　She tells me there is magic
Of such a kind the world dreams not of it.
Ay, magic that would lift a block of granite,

Hid in one form of love. That common magic
Dwells in all things of beauty on the earth,
If we but knew it.

    Diana   Apply this subtle magic, then, to make her well.
                 [Exeunt DIANA and NURSE.

    Goth.   Now, Flavia, what is the cause of this?
    Flav.   There is no cause that I can name to you.
    Goth.   Has it arisen from any act of mine?
    Flav.   No.
    Goth.   What is the cause of all this sickness, then?
    Flav.   Oh, do not ask me! Would I not tell you
If it was in my power?
    Goth.   Why, this is strange!
And have I grown unworthy your confidence
In such a matter?
    Flav.   How I have dreaded this in thinking of it.
Oh, speak of something else, if you still love me!
    Goth.   Love you? I love? Why, this is yet more strange.
And can you doubt? You know how much I love!
Could telling it again add to the strength
Of all the love I have? 'Tis of that kind
That must be dumb; speaking no more with words
Which have no strength to name the shadow of it.
    Flav.   And as you love me, so has been my love;
But as you love me, speak no more of it;
For every time you speak a more than death
Strikes at my heart.
    Goth.   What are these words I hear?
This is most odd. Have I, then, heard you truly?
You, who have sworn to me an hundred times

That you would love me through all time to come,
Like a spoilt child, now say you'll hear 't no more.
   Flav. And if you loved me now you would not speak,
For strongest love stands up above distrust,
So highly honored is the one that's loved.
   Goth. Give me your reasons, though, for this odd conduct.
   Flav. I have no power to give you any reason.
Would I not if I could?
   Goth. Against me nothing should withhold your reasons.
I have the right above all others on earth
To have a reason for your action toward me.
   Flav. I am not well enough to hear you now.
It may seem that I am unkind in this,
But there are reasons, all for some good end,
More bitter far than death, that make me dumb.
Speak of the meeting that was had last night,
Or anything but this.
   Goth. I will obey, and drop this trifling matter.
There was no meeting, for the Emperor's soldiers
Were very skillfully placed there to take us ;
So our good judgment kept us from the place.
   Flav. What hope is there, as things look at the present,
For your success ?
   Goth. Why, a cloudy outlook.
Our strongest allies, taken with sudden fear.
Have been afflicted by a certain quaking ;
Their muscles grown so woefully relaxed,
They would prove useless at a hint of danger.
I look to see their nostrils widened out,
Their eyes stare wide,
And see them shiver as if they had the ague

When danger comes, indeed.   Forgetting now
They once mistook themselves for men of honor,
They break their oaths, and slip away from us.
There's news that's worse, or better far than this :
The Emperor has settled it to-day
(Believing still th' attempt to murder him
Was done by us) that from our band
One shall be chosen within two days
To die for this offense, or all be by him
Considered guilty of it.   Therefore, to-night
We will cast lots to see who is to die.
 Flav.   Oh, cruel ! cruel !   And there's no other way !
 Goth.   Unless some one of us offers himself
The victim for the rest.
 Flav.   Is there no way to lift this odium
Of guilt that rests upon you by proving it false ?
 Goth.   The mightiest proof is still no proof to him
That has his mind fast set the other way.
His fears usurp his judgment ; therefore, no proof
Could ever reach him.   There still is left to us
The choice to fight for freedom till we're dead,
Or, having our rights all dead, live on without it.
But then against a struggle for our rights
Stand forth our timid friends, and ev'n Basilius,
With smooth, persuading words, argues against it.
 Flav   Basilius ?
 Goth.   Basilius.   What of Basilius ?   What of him ?
 Flav.   Nothing.
 Goth.   There's that within your tone speaks more than
  nothing,

And in your eyes I read unspoken words
That tell me more.   You love him !
    Flav.   Gotharva, you shall not speak thus to me.
    Goth.   Tell me ; you love him !
    Flav.   You shall not ; you shall not speak——
    Goth.   Then do not speak, but listen to my words :
Mine is no common love.
My life was built to grow with wars around it.
Though now a slave, I was a soldier once,
And nothing on earth so strengthens the love of honor
As life amid tumultuous scenes of war.
My love is not that kind that women trifle with.
When I gave you my love, without reserve,
I gave you all of it.
And in your hands, that then I deemed most pure,
I placed a sacred trust—more than my life.
And when I told you of it, you took an oath
Before the face of heaven to hold it sacred.
    Flav.   And is it so ?   And must it come to this ?
Oh, Gotharva, and have you even a dream
How deep a wound is made by every word ?
And do you know that words can murder women,
As well as points of steel, where they have loved ?
Will you not trust me but a little more ?
You know my word once given, nothing could break it,
If I must die a thousand times to keep it.
    Goth.   You love me, then ?
    Flav.   Love you ?   Love you ?   No, no ; 'tis more than
      love ;
'Tis something that would make me still cling to you
Through ill report, or 'gainst a world in arms,

And through your own unjust beliefs against me,
Had they no end, on to the end of time.
Thus would I love, were there no reason as strong
To hold me back.

    Goth.   Still, then, you will be mine?

    Flav.   It cannot be.

    Goth.   Then why is this?

    Flav.   I told you that I've lost all power to tell you.

    Goth.   There's contradiction 'twixt your words and acts,
And I am but another sacrifice,
The fool to woman's insatiate vanity.
If Basilius would ask you for your hand,
Your answer would be yes.   Deny me that?

    Flav.   Oh, that my heart would break; that I might
       drop;
That these, my nerves, were dust, to feel no pain!
As you once loved me, do not ask me that.
By the sweet hours that we have had together,
Oh, do not ask me!

    Goth.   I will not ask, for you have answered me.
Perhaps the sweet delusion, though, has served some purpose,
In that it seemed to gratify your fancy.
I see, though, now, that you mistook my nature.
You knew not how I loved; for had you known,
Your pity would have stop'd you long ago.
And had you known that with the love I gave
Went all the earnest part of this my nature,
Went my ambition, all my earthly hope,
All there was of me—then had you known
That, this love ended, all the rest would go,
And leave me all undone.

Flav. Am I not human?
Cannot these words—I will not ask you this ;
But, from the God in heaven, I ask for death.
Oh, Father, look upon my heart and see my prayer,
And knowing alone what's there, grant me relief !
  Goth. Sweet Flavia, how I have loved you !
Let me look in those eyes—a woman's eyes.
Did ever man yet read such eyes aright ?
Gentle as heaven in all their outward view ;
Yet it has been my rule throughout my life
To believe no word that's spoken against a woman,
Whether 'tis true or false—and yet, and yet !
The past is dead, and all my mirrored future
Broke with the mirror that did picture it.
Therefore, to save some life still damned with hope,
I'll give myself up to the Emperor.
  Flav. Oh, God ! You will not !
  Goth. And wherefore should I live,
Since Flavia, while playing with my love,
Has snap'd the chords that answered to its touch,
And all my life has lost its former savor,
And I am now the man I was no more.
  Flav. Since you will have it so, my prayer 's for death :
I cannot live, since you will trust me not,
And will not pity me.
  Goth. Why, yes, I will.
I do not think the deed was charged with malice :
Therefore, I'm sad that you should grieve for it.
  Flav. But say you'll not give up your life ?
  Goth. Why should I live ? You do not need my friend-
    ship ;

For as Basilius loves you, he's your friend.
And for those others, who have been my friends,
I am no more the one to lead them on.
The soldier 's dead within me, and to lead,
One must have hopes as high as heaven itself ;
Ambition that would mount up to the stars,
Searching for fame. All that I had has left me.
Why, I am nothing now,
But something different from the rest of men,
Seeming all out of place—
A shadow only, falling from what I was,
And all my future glides into shadow now.
   Flav. And must it be? And is your love like smoke,
To fade away with every wind that blows?
Ah, me ! How wretched is my woman's fate
That clings to this inconstant love of man—
A love that knows no reason, once 'tis disturbed.
Will you not trust me but a little more?
   Goth. What is there left to trust? Your very words
Tell me you love another. If you love him,
You cannot love me. I have served the plaything
That ferried your thoughts across some tedious hours ;
And is this not enough?
I will not tell you that this was unkind,
For that, at once, would end my long-held dream ;
And then I am too weary grown of late
To utter aught that seems reproaches
'Gainst anything.
   Flav. Oh, if it must be so, God pity me !
Why, could I but speak now the words, I would—
   Goth. Speak no excuse ; 'twere only heavier still.

'Twas only a maiden's fancy, thoughtless as air ;
'Tis all forgiven.   Farewell, Flavia !   ⌊*Exit.*

Flav.   What fearful sin is this that I have done
That such a punishment must follow after
To fix this balance in my growing state
'Till it be ripe to live ?
I cannot live with this !

Scene II.

ARISTEUS, CEPHIAS and HIPPIAS. Enter ARISTEUS, meeting
the other two.

Aris.   What, my old friend Cephias ?   Hippias, too ?

Hip.   Why, as I live, 'tis Aristeus.

Aris.   No other.   And it is good for sore eyes to look
on you both, for it makes real to me the belief that I am
home again.   It pleases me, also, to see in your case, Hippias, the signs of coming success in life.

Hip.   How so ?

Aris.   Fatness and a bald head.

Cep.   When did you arrive ?

Aris.   But an hour ago, and know nothing of what has
occurred in my absence.   Tell me the news.

Hip.   Why, everything is new ; the whole world has
changed and turned about since you left.   Basilius is to be
married, Laarchus is dead, and Gotharva has become so
benevolent that he has presented himself to the Emperor in
order that that august functionary may have the pleasure
of hanging him.

Aris.   And so Basilius is to be married ?   And who is
his particular folly ?

Hip.   He is to marry Flavia.

Aris. Why, I thought Gotharva stood in the way of that ?

Cep. He thought so himself, but having learned his mistake, he became a madman, and commenced traversing the streets with his hair uncombed and his stockings down; smiling to himself bitterly, like a man with a grievance ; repeating snatches of odd phrases. Afterwards he became a philosopher, and became a burdensome nuisance by spouting philosophy to every man that he met.

Aris. Sit down here and tell me all. How is it that he has come under the Emperor's displeasure ?

Cep. Why, not long since the Emperor's life was attempted by some piece of the earth's scum, and the Emperor took the unpleasant notion into his head that the piece of scum referred to was one of our Order. He therefore ordered us either to give up this individual or some other member of the Order (he did not seem to be particular which) to be punished for this offense by death. We held a secret meeting, and looking upon the matter as inevitable, were about to cast lots to determine who was to play Jonah, when Gotharva stept forward and would hear of nothing but he should be the man. As it seemed to be an enjoyable prospect to him, we were generous enough to give way.

Aris. But what was the cause of this in Gotharva ?

Hip. Love did the most of it, and then his vanity was wounded that we would not be as mad as he, and rise up against all odds to strike for freedom. And then it seemed as if the thoughts within him were shaken up and cast a thousand ways by some great grief.

Cep. What would you think to hear

That one who was so rough once in his nature
Had spent an hour talking of charity;
That he had seen
A thousand new things of this charity;
That lack of it but grew from ignorance;
That mightier wisdom made it mightier still,
Till charity was God.
And that if all men on the earth but had it,
Each had a power to heal another's wounds,
And others his.
That if we all and each had charity,
The laws that swayed and ruled the worlds of stars
Would rule this baser earth.
So would we live as brothers, man to man,
Equal in all things then through charity;
An equal right to earth;
For this is but another form of air;
An equal right to air;
For this is but another form of light;
An equal right to light;
For all these three are one.   And then he said,
Having within our hearts this charity,
Laws would be needless and those governments
Would cease to be, which, by their harsh divergence,
Make things unequal.
Thus having brought peace to the minds of men,
The body's ills would pass away forever;
For hatred, envy, anger, evil thoughts,
Each stamp a host of ills upon the flesh;
But heaven's light of charity let through
Will cure us of diseases.

Aris. These words speak not of him as I have known
  him ;
Yet man is oddly odd, and is each moment
Changed by each movement in the universe,
And every sound he hears changes his nature.
Each year he lives he leaves his former self
A stranger to himself,
And is another man each year he lives,
And he that was a villain yesterday
May change to be the noblest of his kind.
And so, when he has reached the end of life,
He sees himself a curious race of men,
Resembling the world around him.

Hip. And has died many deaths—
When grown a boy, the infant that once he was,
That, shedding no tears from out its half-closed eyes,
Strained its young throat in violent, rapid cries ;
That clenched its little fists, wrinkled its brows ;
That squared its mouth, and uttered its angry cries,
Is dead to him, as if it ne'er had been.
When grown a youth, the boy he one time was,
Whose open look concealed a world of mischief,
Who now had grown into that other state,
When all his acts are aping deeds of manhood.
Wading the pond, with pants rolled to his knees,
He sails his ships to distant foreign ports ;
Or, like a youthful engineer, builds bridges ;
Or builds miniature mills by waterfalls ;
Or, in his father's boots and father's coat,
An ancient sword, that drags upon the ground,
Beats on his drum, that swings from side to side ;

A hillock is a battlefield to him.
And then his youthful, uncurbed imagination
Imports him foes enough.   He see their weapons,
Hears in the wind a thousand sounds of war,
Yet marches onward.
Then, when a man the youth that once he was,
With all his dreams, as yet so trusted in ;
With all his glowing fancies, his sudden loves;
Since every woman is a goddess to him ;
His hopes of rescuing them, by gallant deeds,
From desperate straits; from foes imaginary ;
His love of dress cut by the latest fashion ;
His hours spent at the glass ; the care bestowed
Upon his curled moustache, his perfumed hair :
His chafing beneath advice from older heads,
As though it were reflection on his manhood,
His wondrous conceit of youth and knowing air ;—
This being is dead to him of middle life,
When this conceit is crushed out by rebuffs,
And coming wrinkles experiences do mark
Not all o'ercome.   And so, through all these deaths,
These miniature deaths,
These perfect emblems of the death to come,
We still live on.
   Cep.   One of the oddest freaks of all his madness
Is the belief he's found the fabled stone
Of which the world has dreamed these many years.
He says 'tis buried in each one of us,
That if we only would obey its laws,
We would not need to use our earthly senses ;
For then those senses, that are growing in us,

Would show the inmost secrets of all worlds,
And much more madness did he talk to me.
He told me how it was, and why it was,
Two beams from out the ray sent from our sun
Kept the world whirling ever on its axis ;
The manner all worlds are moving, and whither they move.
He said that noble thoughts, born in the heart,
Will wander from it out into the world,
And, like sweet spirits, then tempt other men
To feed and clothe the naked and the poor ;
While evil thoughts rush out into the world
To laugh at right, to make men proud of wrong,
To sneer at good,
And fill men's mouths with windy words against it.
For in one way (the world will one day learn)
This mighty universe is built by faith,
And mountains grow from it.
That day all sects will pass away,
And none be left to pray for us and damn us ;
And all our creed be charity and love ;
That in that day the prisoned would be freed,
And cages used for savage beasts alone.
That yet the time will come
When every man will help the fallen up,
Nor preach to them about the wrongs they've done.

   Hip.   He seems, indeed, to have mingled some sense
with his madness ; but the odd thing is that he says that it
is madness to us, because it is beyond our comprehension—
which is a curious freak for his madness to take.
He says, as well, he had begun t' observe
The wondrous mysteries, passing belief,

Inscribed within the commonest acts of nature ;
That from the basest folly wisdom came ;
That in our dreams we oft recalled events—
Scenes in our lives these thousand years ago.
There is no man on earth but can be great —
As great as any that the world has seen—
If he would but do right each hour he lived.
This was, indeed, the royal road to learning.
I told him, then, the gods did rule our acts ;
He laughed to hear of them, and said
That God was far beyond.
The suns, themselves, were particles of light
In a grand stream of light that still flowed onward.
That all the worlds of heaven were atoms only
Of the one form through which this life-stream flowed ;
Still, this was but one of a world of beings
That had their acts, their duties, to perform,
And they formed but the atoms of a God
Still far beyond. And he had his companions
Looking still upward. Then he took an hour
To tell me how the winds that swept the earth,
The waves of thought, that ruled earth's mental state,
The waves upon the ocean, and all force,
Grew from dividing up the rays of light
That came from our sun and the other suns ;
That all this universe
Was but a mass of struggling, shattered light :
That all these things, by love, were drawn together
Back to their source ;
And that our sun moved on its axis, too,
From west to east ;

That there are laws of gravitation for
Our souls, laws of attraction for our spirits,
In heaven and earth, on to the end of time.
And more he added, which proved him clearly mad.

    Aris. Well, for that matter, each one of us is mad
To some other, and he to us is so,
The only diff'rence 'twixt the sane and mad
Being in the parts they play. And who can tell
But that the mad are wisest of the two?
The fancies of one age, its laughing stock,
Becomes fixed science the next.
Yet nothing 's fixed—not ev'n the granite rock.
All will be overturned,
And what was fancy, then science, must turn to fancy again.
Some mighty thoughts have come to drunken men,
To youth old age seems ever stuffed with folly.
And in the eyes of age youth seems the same.
Who knows but that 'tis so?
To those who went before this age were mad,
And that which is to be to us were madness.
All down the centuries, there 's some one still
To tell us times have changed.
Tell me, how did this madman act
In off'ring up his life?

    Hip. He said he gav't because 'twas worthless to him ;
That once he loved it ; but now these toys of life
Seemed stale and most unsavory to his nature.
Therefore, he wished to die and step beyond
To view the mighty wonders yet undiscovered.

    Cep. The qualities of his courageous nature
Stood all unshaken in the face of death.

When the guards came and placed their chains upon him,
He asked for our good thoughts to swell the sails of death ;
Our thoughts of charity, to calm the ocean ;
Our loving thoughts, to quell the storm he met.
And for his body he asked, when he was dead,
We'd lay 't away in silence,
And let the memory of the deeds he did,
If they be good, be all his monument ;
If evil, then, in pity for his folly,
He begged us not to raise a stone to him,
Lest it should mark them.
Since, in the prison, some fits of violence
Have further showed the nature of his madness.

Aris.   When is 't the sentence is executed ?

Hip.   To-morrow.

Aris.   Why, I must see him, then, at once ;
For though he has met with this great misfortune,
Yet shall not this (as is the common case)
Make me forget that he and I are friends.

SCENE 3.—The Palace of NERO. FLAVIA before the Emperor's throne.

Flav.   And is my urging, then, all without hope ?

Nero.   Hopeless it is, and will not serve your end.
You might beseech, you might still implore,
Adding more to these many arguments ;
My nature is unbending as is iron,
Not to be moved.   When I have once decreed
All hope then ends;   Nothing would change me.

Flav.   And yet my love adds fuel to my hope,
Knowing that greatness does not fear to bend ;
For those I love I know no end to hope.

As 'twas not known Gotharva did this deed,
Cannot I die as well ? Oh, take my life instead !
  Nero. This is the raving madness of your despair.
What purpose were there in taking such a life ?
  Flav. If nothing more, it were a loving deed.
Oh, if you knew what magic medicine
Comes from good deeds to soothe tumultuous lives,
Then would you hear me ;
For every good deed soothes away our fears,
Brings gentle dreams to calm our night's repose,
And smoothes the pathway of our after years.
Have you not felt the tortures of ambition ?
That bitter wormwood 's the rounding up of fame,
Howe'er 'tis sought.   Then must you know 'tis true
That loving deeds bring grandest recompense :
For love is the sweet music of the spheres,
Our highest attribute.   That proudest deeds
Are done through this.   And having love in him,
Man sees beyond these petty bounds of earth,
Learns all philosophy ; for, being in this state,
His nature harmonizes with high moves,
And flashes of truth fall on the world within him.
Having this love, unknown ev'n to himself,
And by an undreamed of chemistry of nature,
His thoughts go to the other ends of earth,
Soothing the broken-hearted, lifting the fallen,
Cheering the weary traveler on his way ;
Still teaching men the cowardice of wrong ;
For love itself is up above all fear.
This being so, were 't not a sweet revenge,
Then, to forgive him ?

Nero.   I see no point to such an argument.

Flav.   Since having this sweet love, each deed we do
Lives after us on to the end of time ?
For never a deed of love was done on earth
But somewhere is remembered,
And love will make all men on earth our friends,
Strengthen us in those offices we hold
While yet we live, and write our names, when dead,
Upon the very walls of heaven itself ;
While rule by force does but excite the strong
To open war ; the weak to secret hatred.

Nero.   Yes ; I have heard such things ; and therefore I
Have heard enough of them, without once more
Hearing them told again.   Therefore, leave off,
For 'tis a waste of time.

Flav.   And when I plead before you for a life,
A human being, moulded like yourself,
That thinks and feels as you, that loves his life,
And finds it sweet to live ;--
Ay, as your life were sweet, were you where he is,
Can you not hear me ?
Has he not friends in whom his love is placed,
And, when he dies, must they not suffer, too ?
Oh, think of this, and do not punish those
So near to him, yet innocent of wrong !
Oh, that I had some higher language still
Then these poor halting words.

Nero.   Since women love a grievance above all things,
And you have that, what more, then, would you ask ?
For if you had the power of Orpheus
'Twould never serve you.

Flav.   My lord, consider how short is this brief life ;
But a few summers and a few short winters added,
And then comes death.
Our enemies die with the breathing moment,
But our good deeds are friends that go with us
On to the end of time.
Who knows but ere the night, we all must die,
And leave behind all wealth, all power and state ?
And if our evil deeds must follow us,
What friend will there defend us,   .
If we have here been friend to none on earth ?
See how death glides on through the world around us ;
Touching the plowman, as he holds his plow ;
Taking the miser, counting, with smiles, his gains ;
The maiden, her dream of love all but accomplished ;
The great inventor, with some mighty scheme,
Would end one-half the sufferings of the world,
Dies with the secret buried in his ashes.
To see ourselves ; how petty our date of action.
Look back at all the ages of the past,
Lost, as a bubble broken ; and the march of life,
And all the beings, more numerous than the sands,
Faded away.   No more substantial now
Than all their fears, their hopes, their deeds, their judgments ;
And those who stand where we stand, ages hence,
Ignoring themselves, and curious of distant things,
Will wonder what we thought, we said, we acted,
And see in us
Some fancy that passed through the brain of earth ;
Some midnight dream of war, of hate and strife.
Oh, since our time 's so brief, let us, then, use it well !

Nero [*to guards*]. Bear her out.
Flav. And yet he shall be freed !
Nero. And, if he is, your head shall answer it.

––––

ACT V.

Scene 1.

Cephias—Hippias.

Cep. Hippias, do you know what I think ?

Hip. No ; your head is too impenetrable.

Cep. I do not remember in all my life an occasion on which I 've done such violent thinking.

Hip. I sympathize with you, as it must have been excessively painful to you. And what do you think that you thought ?

Cep. Why, that we have a mutual friend whose eyes are so nervous that he cannot look one square in the face for two continuous moments. If this were all, it would not matter ; but I have discovered that he has the habit of gazing long and critically at the back of my head. As my head was not made to be the especial object of his criticism, this is unpleasant. And though I do not see him, I feel conscious that there must be an expression of contempt on his features—and it disturbs my bile to think so. I notice, too, that when I talk to him, he seldom speaks, but listens with a silent, contemptuous smile on his face, that seldom leaves it—a most aggravating smile. And on one occasion, while I was explaining to a friend, and was reciting the rules of the critics, to show that epic poetry is superior to dramatic—for so it has been held by the Greeks, those

honored judges—he surveyed me from head to foot, with a
vile smile on his features.

Hip. Why don't you jerk him under the ribs with a
knife, and make him smile aloud ?

Cep. Some day I will.

Hip. Some day, that is another word for never. The
man of action wastes none of his energy in words; but
closes his mouth, his muscles are tightened, his energy is
summoned and the act is performed; and then if he speaks of
it, it is after the deed is done, and with modesty ; but, my
dear Cephias, when you tell us that you will perform a
deed, you warn us that you will not. And so it is with
the woman who tells you that she is going to kill you ; by
assertion she denies it.

Cep. Well, but I must wait to find cause for my quarrel ; for a bare smile is hardly a provocation. He is the
most difficult man to pick a quarrel with ; for he never
loses his temper ; so answers your words of abuse, that it
seems as if he had interpreted them to be compliments ;
and for your abuse he returns civility. And yet his smile,
in the meantime, would stir a saint's bile.

Hip. Tweak his nose, and ask him how he came to have
the impudence to point it at you. That's cause enough.

Cep. You have relieved me at last of a heavy burden.
I shall obey you in every particular.

Hip. Whose nose is it ?

Cep. Basilius'.

Hip. I might have known it by instinct.
He's the most perfect model
To shape all villains by—the world before
Has never seen his like.   [*Shouts within.*

Though without proof,
Yet I am sure he plays the traitor to us.
I feel it in my bones; that never do deceive me.
He sighs too oft, as if his inward nature
Were weeping for the wicked, wicked world.
He has no love for children ; scowls upon them ;
Has no compassion towards the weak and helpless ;
And then his smooth, insinuating language
Comes sweetly through his cruel, murderous mouth.
He lightly ridicules what's honorable ;
Says there's no rule but has an opposite
As reasonable as it.
And then he has not left—no, not a fixed conviction—
His voice, his gait, his looks, and all his acts,
But chiefly his eye, bespeaks him treacherous.

Cep. There you bear me out in my own judgment of him. He is so intensely selfish, that he must be a scoundrel. And there's no mistaking the nature of this cynicism, which I have experienced at his hands. There are men who seem half ashamed of a generous nature, and use cynicism to conceal it; but our friend Basilius cannot be measured by this method, for there is too much of the devil's own venom in his satire.

Hip. 'Tis odd that Flavia would choose him ;
But there's no way, and never will be one,
To mark the lighting of a woman's fancy ;
'Tis governed by no law of heaven or earth.

Cep. Women and death are two odd characters,
And hard to comprehend,

Enter DEMETRIAS.

Dem. What, idle at such a time as this ?

Hip.   At what a time ?

Dem.   Then have you not heard of the glorious news
That shakes the air of Rome ?

Cep.   What news is this ?

Dem.   Why, all the air was pregnant with pent-up
    danger,
And that deep silence of all determined states
Broke, like a hurricane, an hour ago ;
The poorer citizens, soldiers and slaves
Are in a riot.   The Emperor fled this morning,
And I have learned from soldiers just returned
From following him, he died by his own hand.
The Senators have fled in terror,
And many of the rich, bearing their goods,
Were chopped down in their flight.

Cep.   Now is the time,
Then, to release Gotharva from his prison.

Dem.   It is too late ; he has been freed already.
I've seen him in a dozen quarters of the city,
Talking, with words of fire, to crowds about him,
Who list, with breath held close, to catch his words.
He has already got a thousand men
Who'll follow him to any purpose.
Why, here he is, and hundreds crowding after.

        Enter GOTHARVA, followed by citizens,

Goth.   I pity you, but not to make you weep
Like children pitied for some trifling matter,
But for the reason that throughout all time
The poor are over-judged and over-punished,
Seldom are pitied, and over and over betrayed.
I love the poor, the criminals and outcasts

Because they have the harder share of life
Without being worse than those who live in state.
Religions are taught the poor by purchased priests,
And in the name of God and charity
They are instructed Heaven protects the rich
In robbing and in pillaging the poor ;
And that the poor must all be humble still,
For God gave them no rights.
All governments have been made by the rich,
And with the taxes taken from the poor
Have hired their myrmidons, who do protect them
In property they've stolen from the poor.
The rich man breaks no law, having no cause, being rich,
But does a thousand crimes not in the books
More damaging than all those written there
To get his wealth.
I love the poor because they have no friends,
It being my nature in this war for life
To sympathize with every dog that's down.
I love all outcasts, since the world condemns them,
Because the world is all a monstrous lie,
I love all outcasts—women being of their number ;
And since the thousand good parts in their natures
Are not erased by one sole act of wrong.
I'm chiefly their friend because they have no friend ;
Because here, too, the rule is still the same—
From ignorance does come our condemnation.
Because I've seen a thousand good things in them,
And dare maintain it ;
And that the rich commit the selfsame acts,
And are called good and honorable still.

I love all those who 're down, being down myself ;
And know my strength,
And have no chance to use it, while yet fools
Having the accidents of birth to help them ;
Or having that wealth without which they were nothing,
Stand in high places where they 're out of place ;
And all the silly world, being trained to parrot judgment,
Shouts there is room atop for all the great,
And such like catching, idiotic phrases ;
So asses are changed to gods, who spend their time
In studying how they can conceal their folly.
I love the poor because their suffering
Is that alone which is no lie on earth ;
Since I have seen that all laws are so made
(Under some phrase that hides their hidden purpose)
By those in power, having intelligence,
That those who have earth's goods will have more added ;
While those who have but little have it torn from them
By the self-acting power of these laws.
Oh, heaven, if you are men, shall this go on—
On to the roll of doom ?
Will you permit the clogs and stops of habit
To hold you back from seeing what are your rights ?
And will you stand still in the catalogue
Marked with dumb brutes, the common property
Owned by some other dust ?
Must it be still a truth that ev'n the brutes
Assert their rights more quickly than do men ?
But man's odd nature
Does picture ills that are imaginary,

While real dangers pass him unobserved.
Now calmly, silently, as worthy men
Be led by me to ask what is your own,
And you shall have it.
 Cits. Lead us, and we will follow.
 Others. Lead on, Gotharva.
 Goth. Nay, not too fast;
But let me press upon you this is a time—
One of the kind made by the laws of nature—
For some great purpose.
This day our acts shall change men's sentiments,
From whence changed laws will grow. But if you fail,
Full many a day will pass ere comes another
Of such a golden nature. What! Is't possible
That all these faces that I see before me
Are those of slaves and bondsmen! I'd rather be a dog
And have the freedom dogs give each to each
Than be what we are.
 Cits. Lead on!
 Goth. I'd rather far be blotted out forever
Than have within me an immortal soul
Held at the beck and call of things that rot.
 Cits. Lead on! Lead on!
 Goth. Why, this sounds sweetly!
Let danger then make friends of enemies
And strike like men. The very elements
Flee when the brave advance.
Now will we quickly join us with the soldiers,
And then elect an Emperor who shall agree
To give us all those rights which we demand. [*Exeunt.*

SCENE II. FLAVIA sitting, with her head down. GOTHARVA and a physician in another part of the room, consulting together.

Phy. You say that she but seldom speaks to any,
Seems to observe none of the things around her,
Holds her hands clasped, and like a marble image,
Shows naught of animation in her face ?

Goth. Except at times she sighs. At intervals
(Though looking to the front, her eyes unmoved)
She'll talk of things, and disconnectedly,
That are not present, and bear no connection
To things around her. If she speaks of them,
'Tis of some trifle, and she talks of it,
Touching most carefully on foolish details,
Commenting on those points of little note
With serious air ;
Using no judgment 'twixt trifles and higher matters.

Phy. Who was it that was with her through the night ?

Goth. Her friend Diana. I will bring her here. [*Exit.*

Flav. [*Rises and goes to the doctor.*] So, your lordship,
you have concluded to hear me ? But I am weary, weary,
weary with long waiting, and never hear.

Phy. Poor child, you want but a little rest, and you
will get over it.

Flav. No, not here, for they are my enemies ; and I
heard them speaking in the next room of some way to get
rid of me. Have you heard the town crier—I mean during the night.

Phy. No.

Flav. Oh, do not say no ; you know that you must
have heard him.

Phy. What did he say ?

Flav. The town crier?

Phy. Yes.

Flav. Why, who spoke of him? Has any one mentioned him?

Phy. Poor child!

Flav. Have you heard the news? More war, more war! Blood, blood, blood! Do you think they like it? Do you, now? Tell me truly. Can you define the meaning of that cruel word love? It's hard. I mean the true definition. I mean the exact definition—the exact—the exact—the exact—what did I say?

Enter GOTHARVA and DIANA.

Phy. Madam, good morning.

Flav. Good morning.

Phy. [*to Diana*] 'Twas my wish to see you
To ask of you each thing you've noted in her,
Since first this sickness seemed to come upon her.

Diana. Why, she was ever harping on the theme
Of cruel wars, which she called barbarous
And most degrading to the name of man ;
And of the cruelty of massing riches
Beyond the power of using a tithe of them,
Were we as wasteful as the waves of ocean,
Making ten thousand poor ; yet seeing want,
And with our mass of wealth still all untouched,
Letting them suffer still.

Phy. But when was't first
You saw th' approaching signs of madness?

Diana. Why, I was with her during th' exciting day
When Nero fled, and riot was wild in Rome.
With her I watched the houses that were fired,

And saw the angry flames leap up to heaven,
The black and curling smoke dropping its sparks,
Shoved in huge volumes by the moving wind ;
And when some beam or roof fell to the ground
With sound like thunder, dashing upward
A shower of sparks, she 'd turn her head away.
 Phy. But in this was nothing showed an unreasoning
  mind.
 Goth. The end will be the sooner reached by us
Letting her have her way.
 Diana. 'Tis necessary
To tell it in this way to show you all,—
And then it seemed to terrify her most
To see the senseless crowds rushing along,
Trampling to death those that fell in their way ;
To hear their groans, to see th' inanimate dead ;
To hear the distant clash of swords, and all the sounds
That go with such a time. Late in the night,
While sitting with her, first I noticed this :
Her mind was filled with fears, doubts and misgivings,
With dreadful apprehensions. Then I saw,
Mingling with all the terror thus produced,
There was some heavy matter on her mind
Of which she would not speak.
 Phy. What was the first unreasonable act ?
 Diana. Thinking that she was faint, I spoke of food :
But she replied it was a foolish waste
To give her food, for she had been unkind
To all her friends throughout a life of wrong,
And 'twas ordained that as a penalty
She now should die.

Phy. How has she slept?

Diana. But at odd moments, and then uneasily, with her eyes partly open, as if to see half that was going on around her.

Phy. Has she talked much or little?

Diana. At first her thoughts were uttered without break or hindrance, in a constant stream, and without any accompaning expression on her face to explain them.
She 'd rattle on of wars and bloody scenes,
Then stop, and with most fixed and eager eyes
Would gaze upon imaginary foes,
And, threat'ning, shake her fist at the void air;
Then would she speak some disconnected phrase,
A part of something spoken years ago.
Then what struck me as oddest of it all
She 'd swear at me and utter thoughts obscene;
Then, swinging around as sudden as the wind,
She 'd say she saw naught but unkindness
In every one; and thereupon she 'd weep
In low, deep sobs, I thought would break her heart.
Then came a time she dropped into this state
Of woeful dejection,
Of gloomy and fixed silence that seldom breaks.

Phy. She has been overstrained by some great sorrow.
There is some secret that she cannot tell
Which has a hand in this. Her's is a nature
That has some cords as fine as spider's webs,
As sunbeams in an undisturbed lake,
That cannot bear hard words from any one,
And still live on. Her nerves were drawn too fine
To bear the shock giv'n by unkindness. Look what she does.

[*Flavia draws a paper from her bosom, looks on it vacant-
ly and then drops it to the floor. The physician takes it
up and reads.*]

Phy.   Why, this is a writing from her father in which
he commands her to marry Basilius, and not to mention
to a mortal soul this request.   [*To Diana.*] What are her
relations towards Basilius?

Diana.   She is engaged to become his wife.

Phy.   Do you know whether prior to this engagement
she seemed attached to any other!

Goth.   May God forgive me!   I can see it all,
And see that in my wretched action lies
The greater cause of it.   Cursed be the day
When I was born to grow to such a purpose!
Here is, indeed, a mystery of nature
Such piteous things must happen on the earth,
And I be born to play the blindfold part
Which draws the climax.   What's the hope of cure?

Phy.   Since the disease has not been running long
New grooves of thought have not grown fixed in her
Against the ways of reason.   This gives hope.
Her mind is like the earth in Winter time
After some heavy cloud burst over it;
The waters follow a thousand new-made channels,
Which will be followed in after stormy days
If this storm lasts too long and digs them deep.
But man himself can, when they first commence,
Guide them with ease back to their natural course.
There's something in her life before this time,
Her sunny nature, her gentle disposition.
And (though this cannot be depended on,)

There's something in the perfect mould of feature
That helps my hope of cure.

Goth.   Is there no way for me to act?
Oh, why is it we cannot judge ourselves
And on ourselves inflict a punishment
Which by a self-retaliation cures
Those who are injured by our deeds?
Oh, that I might bring suff"ring on myself,
Were it ten times her madness, that would cure her!
What can be done?

Phy.   Nothing is to be done but only this:
Change not the things around her—only those
Which are connected with the cause of it.
Thwart not her wish but when it must be done;
Give her those things that seem to please her most;
Divert her mind in all ways from her trouble;
And if she likes it, play low music to her,
That beats in perfect time, this way to soothe
The vital streams back to their natural course.

SCENE III.—A graveyard. Two gravediggers boring a hole.

1st Dig.   Brutus!—Brutus, I say!

2d Dig.   Speak louder, man; your voice is getting weaker every day. I see signs of mortality coming over you.

1st Dig.   My voice is strong as it was when I was twenty. The trouble is that your ears are wearing out. I'd be willing to stake the best coin that I have that when you come to die your ears will go first.

2d Dig.   It's a bargain, and the bet's made. Remember, I'll have no backing down; you must stand up to it like a man, and down with the dust.

1st Dig.   I'm a man of my word, and the bet stands,

unless you call it off. Never fear me. But the trouble is
you'll never live long enough to claim the stakes.

2d Dig. Don't you fret about that. All of my family
were long lived, and none of them have died under a hundred, except my youngest child, the cause of it being that
he had black hair, and not auburn hair like the rest of us.

1st Dig. Is that a sign of long life ?

2d Dig. A sure sign, written in the medicine books.

1st Dig. I think that is no sign, though the books do say
it ; for I've planted many a young corpse with light hair.

2d Dig. What an audacity you have, Cicero, to deny
what's wrote in books. They contain all the knowledge,
and can't be wrong.

1st Dig. It don't matter ; the color of the hair is nothing. I always go on the shapes of the skulls. Look at
my skull, and feel it. There's the shape to last. I'd be
willing to stake a fortune on it for long living.

2d Dig. There's nothing in skulls ; and therefore
there's nothing in yours.

1st Dig. I suppose because it's not found in books,
Brutus. Books are but graveyards for stinking thoughts.
But real graveyards are the places to learn.

2d Dig. I say, Cicero, where do you suppose the breath
goes when their toes turn up?

1st Dig. Well, Brutus, there seems to be a good number of different opinions on that subject. Some say it takes
shape and goes up to live with the gods. Others that it
slips into the belly of an infant, or a dog, or a horse, and
grows up to be a man or a woman ; though you don't seem
to know that you have been here before.

2d Dig. Then Pompey and Cæsar, who afterwards

fought like cats and dogs, may have dug graves , and you and I may become great warriors one of these fine days, and fight each other—and oh, won't I wallop your greasy pate when it comes ! But I think it can hardly be. For look at these weak-minded skulls about here—what a booby grin is on them ! How mum they are—how helpless in expression ! I don't think they could ever amount to anything.

1st Dig. There is certainly a very solemn expression about a skull's face; but I speak of the mind, which is in the head.

2d Dig. But where's the man can prove it's in the head ? At times I've thought it was all over ; at other times I've thought it was in my belly ; and then again I've felt it in the fore toe of my left foot. So the question to be settled, Cicero, is, where am I ?

1st Dig. You're but an ass, Brutus, without book-learning. When you cut your toe off does your mind go with it ? No ; you go on talking just the same. Cut your head off and you stop talking, which shows the mind to be in the head.

2d Dig. Cut the tongue off, and you stop talking ; which, by your rule, would show it to be in the tongue.

1st Dig. It's a well settled rule, by the books, that in arguments you are not to come down to fine points, for if you did it would knock all learning into a cocked hat. If you come down to fine points, I can prove there is no mind at all. But no one has a right to be too fine in such matters.

2d Dig. Well, show us there's no mind.

1st Dig. Chop a man's arms off; he still lives ?

2d Dig. Yes.

1st Dig. Cut his two legs off ; he might still live ?

2d Dig. Yes.

1st Dig.   Put plugs in his ears ; he can't hear !

2d Dig,   Yes.

1st Dig.   Put his eyes out ; he can't see ?

2d Dig.   Yes.

1st Dig.   Cut his tongue off; he can't taste !

2d Dig.   Yes.

1st Dig.   Spoil his nose ; he can't smell ?

2d Dig.   Just so.

1st Dig.   Then, as he can't taste, hear, smell or see, he can't think.   As he don't think, he don't have a mind. But yet he lives.   See ?

2d Dig.   It do look reasonable—but here they come with the body of Flavia.

1st Dig.   Flavia ? Is that the name ? How did she die ?

2d Dig.   Of madness.

Enter funeral train, a priest, GOTHARVA, BASILIUS and others.
The coffin is placed on rests.

Priest.   Here lies the end of love, of hope, of all things
    earthly.

In this poor picture of the one we loved,

Lies the deep mystery men will never solve;—

Beyond all scrutiny and prying looks.

Here in the awful silence of a life that's ended ;

Of sweet affections frozen dumb by death ;

Of ears that will not hear us when we speak ;

Of all the things of yesterday stopped in their course ;

Man's intellects rebuked, and dares no further,

Or going further, ends in worse than nothing.

Here lies a syllable

From the high eloquence of heaven itself,

That's spoke in words too high for man to know :

Here, on this border line where all turn dust,
Is God's own lesson of equality ;
And in this lastest scene of all the acts,
Symbols are found most wonderful of all—
The grandest mysteries of the universe—
To be gazed on and still unlearned forever
In this one-sided life.
Oh, poor dumb lips ! Would you would speak to us ?
But, no, those lips must never move again ;
Yet they were sweet interpreters of heaven.
Oh, why is it that in this world of woe
The good and bad die equally alike ?
Seeing the good might help the ignorant ;
Yet death may touch them through a breath of wind,
So shadowy are the last of earthly things.
Oh, poor cold eyes ; the heaven that shone through them
Withdraws its light, and leaves them staring at earth
As if they knew 't no more. I will not speak,
As is the common custom, of her virtues,
For they were such as needs no one to tell them ;
And as all knew her, loved her, none will deny them.
Therefore remains but one thing to be done ;—
To place this faded flower gently away ;
And from that on, it is my firm belief
That all the gentlest things found on earth,
Obeying nature's laws, will tend her grave.
If sweetest flowers grow not upon it, gentle winds
Will be drawn there to murmur over her ;
And sweetest birds will sing their carols there.
Yet, when I think how much we all have loved her,
How cold and icy seem these words of mine—

For she was one of whom no words can speak ;
Nobler than words can tell—a subject, rather,
That like the grander stars yet undiscovered,
Have beauties unseen, beyond our present description,
She had that deep, that higher charity
Founded upon a deep insight of nature,
On higher wisdom than common mortals have—
She saw that link that bound all things together,
And saw that man depended on the worm
That he might still exist.   Therefore was she
Most gentle to each creature on the earth.
But then her sorrows came too heavy on her,
And all the million things she was but yesterday,
Is now turned to dust.   Oh, place her with the dust,
Give her back to the earth from whence she came —
For I can speak no more.
Silent herself, let silent lilies grow,
The daisies and the violets above her,
With their sweet faces ever looking upward :
Sweet monuments, pointing where she is gone :
The varied hues the sunlight writes upon them,
Being nature's words, telling by loveliest symbols
The qualities once in her.   [*Coffin is lowered into the grave.*
  Goth.   [*Springs at Basilius and stabs him.*]
But for that smile he might have still lived on.
Now let him die, and may his agony
Be greatest ever suffered by man yet.
    Priest.   My son !   My son !   What fatal act is this ?
    Goth.   Speak to me not.   I go to my account.
The drug that acts within me, playing the jailor,
Hurries me on to that dark tribunal —   [*Falls dead.*

DREAM OF REALMS BEYOND US.

A DREAM OF REALMS BEYOND US.

A DRAMA.

ACT I.

SCENE.—A level space on the evening clouds over the Golden Gate. Tents of clouds of gold and silver are seen on the plain. A throne composed of the hues of the rainbow on which rests a spirit named Elmo. Other spirits around the throne.

Etheria. Beloved, commanding spirit, I have obeyed,
In all respects, your dear commands.
Seizing my silvery staff, and placing therein
Sweet thoughts to be attracted westward,
Around the world, back to some other thoughts
Held by you here, I sped upon my mission.
The day I left behind me, outrunning the sun,
And entered the towering palace of the dark,
That through all time stands opposite the sun.
I then swept through its curious moonlit halls,
And there I met those hideous impish sprites
That ever dwell within the tower of night,
That circles the earth as shadow of the sun.
I found them ever mingling the elements,
Making compounds to thwart the course of nature.
From them I learned but little of these beings

That dwell in contact with the earth below us :
But when I overtook the blue of the morning,
I found some beings from a distant sphere,
Larger than mountains, resting in their ships,
That ride the seas of space ; observing these beings
With curious magic instruments they had prepared,
By mixing good and evil in certain proportions,
From them I learned, these beings crawling the earth
Did seem to have a certain intelligence :
And seemed (though roughly), governed by some laws.
While gazing on these insects of the earth,
They said they noted oft they moved in masses ;
At times in order ; at other times without it.
At times they saw two masses move toward each
Slowly and as determinedly as insects,
Yet, there appeared no object in these acts.
But as the blue of dawn changed to that hue,
In which the latter day does dress herself,
These beings could no longer stop near earth ;
Therefore unmoored their ships, and on a rising storm
Swept off through space back to their home again.
 Elmo. Learned you no more?
 Etheria. 'Twas all I learned.
    [Enter ETHRON.]
Here comes a gentle spirit whose bright face
Bespeaks more knowledge.
 Ethron. To learn if these odd beings on the earth
Were living creatures and intelligent,
I called a mighty host of brighter spirits
From all the corners of the universe,
And found amongst them some could see this earth.

They told me that these beings ne'er rose from it,
But moved through shade and light upon its face.
That all their actions showed fantastic thoughts ;
Showing these beings
As very infants in the grades of life,
With little thoughts and monstrous prejudices,
That they were blind and dumb to other worlds,
And knew but monstrous little of themselves.
They said they'd seen small spirits of the light
Dancing around them to the rythmic motion
Of undulating heat on summer days.
Yet men were blind and could not see them ;
And then they told me that the genii of caverns
Would light strange lights, whose flickering flames
Were made by trembling to play melodies ;
Yet they seemed deaf and did not hear these sounds.
They said that those who sailed across the deep,
Seemed not to see th' ocean's inhabitants,
Who, rushing through the air, created storms,
And left their white tracks foaming on it's face.
Men seem like fishes dwelling in the deep ;
Oblivious to those beings that are above them.
That by the deeper concentration on
The faces of some, they thought they all were deaf.
This much I learned :—no more.

  Elmo. Is there no other that has studied them ?
  Blanta. This day I seized on the returning ray
Of the revolving light from sun to earth.
I passed the point these opposite rays do cross,
And sitting along upon
The foremost promontory of the sun,

I watched the silvery earth as it revolved,
Gazed on its star-like pointed atmosphere,
And yet learned nothing of them.
    Elmo.   Since this is then a real race indeed,
And not, as once we thought, but moving plants,
'Twere well for us to better their condition,
By whispering them of higher things.
Has any other of this company
Brought knowledge of this new discovered race?
    Arno.   I have for fifteen circlings of the sun,
Dwelt opposite to him in midnight darkness.
And being unable to go close to earth,
Have forced the beings of night t' obey my orders,
And fetch me information of these creatures.
And first and foremost of their news,
They told me that these beings throughout the night
Seem in a state of death ; but come to life,
Awaking with the wave of harmony,
The sun plays on the rolling lyre of earth.
I then learned that they're often much tormented
By these same beings that I forced to serve me,
And still other devilish sprites,
That, like the skates and mudfish of the ocean,
Dwell near the bottom of the seas of air.
Still other's, too,
Oft tempt them from high cliffs; and often lead them
To their own ruin, placing in their way
Most deadly tempting things.   And then, besides,
Hideous small goblins dwelling in the moon,
Distill into her rays things poisonous,
Which madden them, or give them curious dreams.

And so it is the harassments of earth
Stamp haggard looks, and marks of care upon them.
They scarce are born before the wants of earth
Mark wrinkles on their working infant brows;
And so begins a life of groans and sighs,
Caused by their pains, their wracks and their diseases.
Although 'twas hard to learn, I have discovered
Through pictures shown to me of these mortals,
There's something good in them ;
They seem superior in some trifling points
Over the other animals of earth.
Some acts of theirs, instinctive of their natures,
Those balance points which dot the face of nature
Are exponents of higher qualities.
I saw with them, that love outlasted death;
The strength of mother's love, that's not of earth,
That those who had the least were charitable ;
And being the nearest to their state of nature,
Most charitable.
I saw an infant suck its mother's teat,
Gazing up at her face with loving eyes.
I saw that they wept more o'er other's sorrows,
While their own ills they bore with smiling patience ;
Methinks 'twould be a pleasant thing indeed,
To start this seed of good to growing in them.
    Elmo. It shall be done. Now, for the present time,
We'll have our workmen in the shops of air,
So to combine and forge the elements
That the bright song of twilight shall be formed
Ere sinks the sun to his cloud-curtained bed,
And to that end

Let them combine the light that's shot from Venus,
The color of the ocean's wave by moonlight,
The light reflected from the ocean's teeth,
While angrily she gnaws the edge of the earth,
The dancing atmosphere of summer evenings,
The dizzy moving borealis light,
The weird shadows of gloomy ancient forests,
Whose moss-grown limbs seem like the coffined dead.
The lulling sound of dripping unseen waters,
The grander roar of mighty cataracts,
The sounds like human voices in the woods :
Then all the movements of the hurricane,
And wind up with th' odor of summer's air,
When every flower is dressed in glittering dew :
Its gaudy dress worn on that grand occasion,
When comes the bow of promise, the storm being o'er
To these sights will we dance.

ACT II.

SCENE.—A California forest high up in the mountains. A small
stream is winding through the woods.

Enter DE PETZY and BLAUVELT.

Blau.   Here let us rest and make our camp to-night :
And let our tired limbs and aching bones
Be patients for a time to such attendants
As nature sends in shape of cooling winds,
Which, to the patients placed beneath their care,
Bring balmy odors from the waving pines,
Fetches medicinal breaths from ferns and mosses,
And many an herb till we are healed again.

De Pet.   I think we could not better our condition
By going further on.   Besides the night
Now smothers up the glowing light of day,
And ere an hour will quench his light,
And blot this day from off the calendar.
  Blau.   Drop then your gun and rest upon this bank.
How sweet this air ; the gurgling of the stream !
There's something soothing and refreshing to me
To find myself afar from human cares.
Far off beyond the sounding of an echo
Of giant mills, and cities soot begrimmed ;
Our sole companions these dumb trees that stand
Holding behind their grim and solemn aspects
The secrets of a thousand passing years,
Known to themselves alone ; the antlered deer,
Owls whose wise looks tell of their secret knowledge,
And other beasts spell bound ; made dumb by nature,
To hold the wondrous things that they have seen.
Why here's a country to be new discovered !
One of earth's many realms but brushed by dreams.
  De Pet.   Ofttimes, my mind being in a curious mood,
Life seems more like a dream, than ever a fancy
That strode the stage of sleep.   Is it not odd,
Our being fast upon this piece of earth,
That floats a bubble on the seas of space ?
This being our lot, seems a disordered dream ;
A state of odd enchantment that of earth,
While real things are all unknown to us.
  Blau.   I've often thought something more worthy men,
Was hid beyond this childish race for wealth ;
This most absurd expending of a life ;

That in the world was something beyond its sights,
And in the forest something beyond the wolf,
The panther stepping with his cautious tread
O'er crackling twigs in this grim forest ;
The gurgling streams, the silver trout
Whose backs rebuff the kindness of the sun ;
The feathered carpenter, who at his work
So oft deceives th' unwary traveler ;
The grizzly striding here with kingly tread ;
Why, we've but touched the surface of earth's secrets,
Wonders astonishing and unimaginable
Being yet unknown.

 De Pet. There's surely pleasant contrast in these woods,
For, being alone, we have no enemies,
Being far away from all the race of men ;
But having none to hate us, we have not
A mark for gentle thoughts to draw them forth.
Therefore, a life apart from all mankind
Is one that's selfish and unnatural—
The refuge of cowards ; 'gainst love and reason both.

 Blau. List to the cooing of the unseen dove ;
I wonder if they, too, have woes of love—
Heave mighty sighs ; then, with disturbed visage
And eyes grown mournfully large, do gaze upon
Those whom they love, with passionate, pleading looks ?
I wonder, too,
Does she then cast her eyes down with disdain,
And he then misinterpreting this act,
With foolish haste fall a-despairing ;
Then, seeing his deep despair, does she grow kind
But for a time, to end his present grief,

A little later to seem cold again,
And so the action and reaction go
On to the end ? And are they jealous like men ?
With glittering, feverish eyes and visage wan,
Disturbed by trifles, beneath a madman's notice ;
And have they friends, or foes, or foolish customs,
To break sweet nature's course and make love hopeless ?

    De Pet. Why sure it is they have their share of woes,
Wrought chiefly by fear,
Being subject to a life of false alarms :
Mourn for their friends, and in their sweetest songs
Repeat their grief into each other's ears.
But I will leave you now to lonelier musings
And wander off t' explore the woods around us.

       [Exit De Petzy.   Blauvelt lies down and goes to sleep.
      [Enter Wavra and Ellock, two spirits of the woods.]

    Wav. He lies asleep. I'll breathe upon his face,
And by my breath infuse my nature in him,
As lovers do, when breathing each on each ;
Creating such fancies and such odd conclusions
As never yet were lodged in mortal mind.
Then shall he sweep the universe with thought,
And stand amazed indeed to see the things
Pierced by his eye of reason.

    Elmo. Is 't not against Etheria's commands—
Who, for the part she takes in that great work
That now is brewing in the higher heavens,
To help the world on,
Would bring these two together ?

    Wav. Not if such thoughts are placed within his brain
That they are higher than human.

And yet 'twere pleasant, if we had our way,
To make his mind grow drunk with hideous fancies :
But as we are commanded otherwise,
I'll let him in his dreams tread upward,
And being the hero of his deeds of sleep,
Go onward through full many a wondrous realm,
Where waking mortals could not be and live.
I'll show a thousand varied scenes in hell,
And there the laughter in a woman's eyes
Shall end his peace forever.
I'll show the green and monstrous angular sprites
That in the chilly southern seas of ice,
Where shines the southern cross, control the waters
And make the choppy sea dash icy waves
Against the mighty towers and domes of ice,
Full many feet in air ;
That drag the howling winds from point to point,
Shrieking as if in pain ;
That lead these deadly winds against the ships,
Icing the rigging, freezing the sailors' thumbs ;
Then drops the white fogs on the waste of waters,
And all the while so various are the sounds :
The loud reports, the rattling of floating ice ;
That hell itself seems there to have an echo.
I'll show the fourteen stars west of the cross,
Where dwell the dreaded mutineers from Venus.
I'll show the cloud bound caves of distant realms,
Where roam forever spirits of wild beasts.
And then I'll show the wild north central heaven,
Where come the poisonous winds from ev'ry point
Named on the compass ; mingling their poisonous breaths —

The hell of Saturn.
His fancy I'll lead through endless vales of clouds;
To lands whose sun shines with a ray of blue;
Whose stars are green, and all the things that grow,
A dreary white. I'll so astonish his fancy
That waking, he will rub his eyes to see
If he be yet awake.
    Elmo. But then the other one will soon return,
    Wav. No, for he was enticed to taste an herb
O'er which I spread a gauzy spiritual charm,
And now the sun, which is upon his right,
He sees upon his left; and tiny fairies
Paint strange delusions on the air before him,
And laugh and lead him on. So let us hence,
And by our wishes bring the maiden here.
            [*Exeunt. The music of a harp heard within.*
           Enter SYLVIA.
    Syl. Why, who is this, that, in these distant woods,
Lies either asleep or dead? Thank heaven 'tis sleep!
For no death damp does rest upon that brow,
Nor are the eyes sunk back upon the brain;
The rosy proof of life is on his cheek—
Death has not plucked it thence,
And fairy zephyrs steal across his lips,
To leave their gifts of life and then depart;
The while his heart beats steady time and music,
To which the world of life within him moves.
'T were pity, too, for such a one to die,
For honor's written on that lineless face;
The royal stamps of truth and courage,
Those higher marks than all rewards of fame,

More to be valued than the western ocean,
Its face all paved with gold.
And pride that would not beg;—no, not e'en woman's love,
So highly honored were the one he loved.
His brow is curved like heaven on summer days,
And lips to send forth streams of music
Would charm the passions of a multitude
As oil the ocean's anger.
　　Blau. [*Wakens.*] Where am I? Ah! I do remember.
What's this? The glamour of new acquaintanceship?
Or is it yet a sweeter vision still?
Am I awake?
Can fairies blush and turn their heads away?
I feel like one that's drunk, and lift my brows,
Yet cannot lift my eye-lids high enough
To see if this is real. And if 'tis real
It were enough to make one drunk with pleasure!
Why I could gaze, and hold my breath and gaze
And still look on until the world were ended.
And in so living, lose all recollection
Of pain upon the earth?
　　Syl. How came you here?
　　Blau. For twenty miles, I have come here afoot.
　　Syl. Do you not fear to sleep in this deep forest,
With wild beasts round you?
　　Blau. Do you not fear to walk here in this forest
With no protector?
　　Syl. I do not know of fear:—and what is fear?
　　Blau. Fear is that something which comes over us,
When reason is abandoned;
Something that makes us lower than the beasts;

A thing that's loathsome to the highest minds,
As loathsome as dishonesty,
And most controls those most degraded.
 Syl. I've often met the beasts that roam these woods
But looking on them, with the eye of friendship,
They turned away and never offered harm,
And for protection
I have no friends in all the wide, wide world,
But the sweet stars that cheer me with their looks,
The flowers wild, the spirits of the wind;
Those spirits that build pictures in the music
When I have played harp here in the woods,
And oft I while away the summer hours
By watching mighty cities in the clouds,
That passed away ten thousand years ago ;
And those mysterious beings, strangely accoutred,
That pace along the outer battlements ;
The spirits of serpents and of curious beasts
That dwelt in swamps these centuries ago ;
And as they pass in panoramic view.
I live where'er I will in past or future,
Forgetting the present.
 Blau. Have you no mother? Have you no father either,
No sister nor a brother ?
 Syl. I live with those who say they are my parents :
But then, one day, I learned it was not so ;
And who my father and my mother are
I cannot tell : for far as I remember
I've been with them here in these woods alone ;
And for companions—they have kept me from them,
They make me work from morning till the night,

And beat me when I'm tired and cannot work ;
And if they are away, they set a dwarf,
Who's cruel and malicious in his nature,
To watch my acts.   But when he is asleep,
Then I steal forth and wander in the woods ;
But if he awakes before I do return,
He seizes me and beats me cruelly ;
Grinning and showing his teeth, and laughing harshly
With brutal pleasure ; but I never weep
And never can they tell from how I look
How much the pain I feel.   Oft seeing this,
I've seen him stirred to madness in his malice,
And in his angered state the poisonous foam
Grew white upon his lips ;
Yet never a muscle twitched to show my pain,
And never a sign betrayed me.
  Blau.   And never a friend to help ?
  Syl.   I never saw a stranger in these woods
But you alone.   Oh, if 1 knew the way,
How quickly would I seek those far off cities
Of which I've dimly heard ; where are great kings
And mighty lords and ladies and courtiers !
  Blau.   Though from your forms we might mistake your
    nature,
And think you were an angel come from heaven—
And though your nature must be still as sweet—
Those thoughts of baubles betray your woman's nature.
Know that there are no titles in a land
Where all are more than kings.
  Syl.   I have seen pictured in my dreams, these cities
Where towers and steeples rose up to the sky,

And old cathedrals on whose marble floors
Fell dim and colored lights.
   Blau.   These dreams of yours
Are not such dreams as city maidens have,
Disturbing their nights.
   Syl.   But hush! Rhadagavat is coming,
And I must leave you.   [Exit Sylvia.
   Blau.   Why here's a romance found within these woods
To shame the dullness of a written book ;
To bring an incredulous sneer quick to the lips
Of men whose sense is not uncommon but common.
No writer's dream, no freak of childhood's fancy ;
No drug-induced imaginings of men,
But pale before this most audacious nature ;
Seeming most tame indeed ;
And seeming unnatural in the face of nature.
                          [*Gun-shot heard.*
             [Enter De Petzy.]
Safe, back again ? What have you learned ?
   De Pet.   I have seen nothing ; neither have I heard
Aught but the wind that rustled the forest leaves ;
And set those limbs that rested against others
To utter doleful moans. Naught but the squirrels,
That high aloft did hold betwixt their paws,
The food they nibbled, careless of my presence ;
But now, I shot this rabbit I bring with me ;
Who sat, with ears erect, gazing upon me,
Then throwing back his ears, started to flee ;
When, pulling the trigger, I ended all his hopes,
Cut his ambitions, checked his evil thoughts ;
But let us hence, for I have found a place

Better than this to make our camp to-night,
Still higher up the stream.

———

ACT III.

SCENE. Same as Scene I, Act I.

Elmo.   Since it has been resolved by us, to each
Help on some being of the human race,
Let those who have observed them give the news.

Eth.   Beloved spirit, it being against our natures
To come in closer contact with the earth,
Since deadly vapors rise from murderous deeds,
And slimy odors rise from cruel acts,
From brutal words, from selfish vanity
Which raises some upon the woes of others :
Therefore I've sought out spirits that have power
To walk upon the surface of the earth,
Of which are multitudes with various natures,
I chose the laughing spirit of the woods
To serve my end.

Elmo.   How learned you from them

Eth.   The air below is filled with finest dust ;
With this they modeled forth a beauteous maiden
And then by casting sunlight on this form,
She seemed to live ; and by this form of hers,
I knew how outward nature acting on it,
Would make her inward mind ; and saw that she
Was one it would repay us well to serve.

Elmo.   How would you serve her ?

Eth.   Why, I have seen this cruel thing on earth
That natures that are fitted each for each,
With bitter hearts—and yet they know not why--

Oft lead a life that's all unsatisfied,
Because they feel and yet they do not know
The other lives for them ; yet die and never meet.
Therefore I've brought the one most fitted for her,
And they have met, and in a moment felt
What, if 'twere told, would crowd these many years.
To consummate my plans.
I've had her flee her home within the woods,
And to prevent her guardians following her,
Have given the spirits under me the power
To play such tricks as pleased them most upon them,
And making then the most of such permission,
They have deluded them to strange beliefs,
And set the men stroking their beards,
Being angrily perplexed ; and on their faces
Expressions ludicrous.
They lead them long journeys through briers and thorns,
O'er angular rocks, through swamps, through wild grapevines,
Oft make one think the other Sylvia,
And set a beating t' other.
I now shall lead her on through trouble and woe,
To find reward at last.
    Elmo.   Has she no earthly friend to help her ?
    Eth.   My servant spirits showed an aged man,
Who childless stood near to the end of life,
Thinking the daughter that he one time had
Was dead in infancy.   They told me then
This was the father of our Sylvia.
I watched his brain, and of the world of spirits
(Which men call thoughts) held fast within his brain,
I saw 'mongst others these, his last conclusions,

Which showed some odd things of the race of men :
All pleasures bring reacting torments with them,
Being balanced with an equal weight of care ;
Debauchery brings the thought of suicide,
Placing the strong in hell, o'ercoming cowards.
Nothing is valued but what others have—
Children and men being both alike in this—
Envy enraged then at another's fortune
Gives value even to a worthless thing,
Great as the trouble had in getting it ;
Riches so madly sought, strike dead to friendship,
Oft chill and oft debase
The hearts of those that get them ;
And yet the parasitic natures of mankind
Lead them to still bow down before this wealth,
Though past all chance of benefit from it.
Riches are traitors
That bringing many pleasures surfeit with all.
And so this everlasting yearning in us
Falls short the mark 'tis aimed at.   I saw besides,
The leaders of the world work by no rules,
But at their birth come new rules to the world,
Shown by their deeds.   But common men
Like sheep are fixed, held down, bound by example,
And follow those that at the moment lead them.
As these thoughts passed his brain, he heaved a sigh.
And then I saw that mortals did not know
To rid us of ourselves and live for others,
Is the one road that leads to happiness.
Therefore, I thought 'twere sweet to prove to him,
That where we seem bound fast and held by fate,

That even then relief will surely come,
If we stand forth all dauntless to the end ;
And ever comes in some path plain enough,
Yet which we had completely overlooked
And lost all memory of.

    Elmo.   This is a good commencement for an end,
To round up royalty.   What other spirit
Would speak to us of what they have observed ?
Here comes a spirit with laughing, impudent eyes ;
Eyes that might find strange humor ev'n in death.

    Fonra.   I've seen their life 's indeed an odd conceit,
Made up of odd conceits.
Seeing the future is but night to them ;
Those who get freely spend as easily ;
Some have the name of being generous,
Who borrow freely and as freely spend ;
Yet all the things they have and half their honor
Is measured but by gold ; and in their hearts
The blood runs cold as ice.
The gold of those who save all that they get
Seems to impregnate and grow to their bones ;
And they,
Like rats and vermin, hide their wealth away,
And ever dreaming that they must live on,
Die ere it is enjoyed.
Some spend their lives seeking to reach that point
When they will stand above those who have scorned them ;
And if 'tis reached, they reach it but to learn
That folly urged them on.
I noted that men were often such low bred blackguards,
They would repeat the tales they'd heard of women,

Or build up lies and slanders of whole cloth,
Which served to damn full many an honest wife.
Women are dazzled most by vice in men,
And pitying their infirmities, do love them.
The tale of love like children they will hear,
And never tire in hearing it repeated ;
And many more mad quirks I did observe
In their odd natures.
The child looks forth with anxious eyes to manhood,
On through the magic windows of the future,
Which show them things that never come to pass
As they are seen at first.   Yet in the picture
That's shown of manhood, they see most wondrous things,
Till reaching it,
They learn manhood's but childhood grown less free
With larger toys to play with.
Oft at the end of life,
Embittered by full many woeful mishaps,
Men gaze back now with melancholy visage,
And bitterly relate o'er to some friend
How life has been a failure ;
Sighing they cannot be a child again
To try 't anew.   This too I've seen of them ;
They're never all good nor not entirely bad ;
But at some times the worst of them are saints,
And then at times the best of them are devils.
The great at times seem small, and then at times,
Those who before seemed insignificant,
Called by some great occasion, take the lead,
An do astonish those who under-judged them ;
And of things or beings animate,

There's nothing on earth half so uncertain,
So little to be depended on as man.
And so this curious race
Would seem to be bewitched by their odd natures,
Could I relate the thousand contradictions
I have observed in them.
    Elmo.   What knowledge have they
Of all the myriads of living worlds around them?
    Vonra.   They are so puffed up by their strange conceit—
Though on a fly-speck of the universe—
That still they think the rest was made for them,
And that no other living being at all
Dwells in the wondrous hosts of worlds around them;
But all is glitttering death, and nothing more;
Made but for them to gaze on through all time
With open mouth, and eyes stretched wide with wonder.
Being fixed to earth, 'twas laughable indeed
To note their knowledge is but halves of things;
They see no interlacing of all things
Between two worlds to make a mighty end,
And all their seeing only is inch deep.
They scarce conceive that all the things of earth
Are things in miniature of full-grown worlds.
That as their nations think and act like men,
At times being sane, at times being mad as they,
So is their race a unit of vast worlds.
That as their seas have puny storms upon them,
So are there storms that sweep the seas of space;
Creating vast currents, whirlpools and tides;
Setting worlds dancing on their rising billows
Like corks upon the ocean.

Sweeping vast systems o'er that mighty deep,
With billows hurrying, rushing, raging onward,
That dash against the beacon lights at night,
And surge beyond.   They dream not of the fleets
That, sails all set, dash o'er the darker ocean
Into strange ports in other realms
Beyond the realm of suns ;
Into those systems held by other checks
Than earths and suns.
Nor will they yet believe
Their brains are but a temporary home
For spirits of dead things upon the earth ;
That they had power that chained these ghosts of thoughts
Fast to all books and ancient monuments.
They laugh at goblins fast in ancient halls ;
That in straight lines walk through dense crowds of men ;
The sooty spirits crouching on storm brewed clouds ;
The airy cities which we all have seen ;
The mighty deserts in the realms of space,
And all the wondrous hosts of distant heavens ;
Looking within, they seem to see these things ;
But looking out upon the sun again,
They call them fancies, and they vanish from them.
These things they will not know, and do not know ;
And hearing it, they call 't unreasonable,
 Elmo. Ah, if they could but know the half we know !
How would it shake their minds and make them mad ?
Being so unreasonable.
 Vonra. Their chiefest cause of all is ignorance,
From which springs prejudice and every folly ;
This shadow of death is now most heavy on them.

But with our aid, the world begins to move.
This century does promise mighty times
That will out leap the tedious course of nature ;
Leaving behind the barbarous days of war ;
Of right by blood to be the manger dog ;
Of rights devine, and many another right
That always has been wrong.
The time will then come to this human race,
When men will say there is
No aristocracy but that of honor.
And he alone will be a king amongst them
That has this honor.
For men will learn that time; that true it is
To be the mightiest man the world e'er saw,
And have not honor, were indeed as nothing ;
For honor's the salt and savor of true greatness
In men and nations both—their sustenance.
For what's called greatness
That has not honor's, but a sickly growth
To droop and fade, and pass away forever.
But nothing on earth's assured so long a life,
Repeated by men, and filling their memories
Through coming ages, as deeds of honor and right.
    Eth.   There's this thing to remember as excuse.
How much they're ruled by fate
Down in that earthly hell.
Their life from infancy on to old age
Being but the lived and acted history
Of that same earth they dwell on,
In each minutest act through all her course.

Elmo.   Know they the heavenly character of music,
Whose words are founded on a common language,
Inscribed in which are secrets of all worlds
Throughout the heaven ; which the higher powers
Read at their pleasure.
  Eth.   'Tis sweet to them ; but that it is a key
Made to unbolt the gates of heaven,
They do not know.
  Elmo.   Odd, odd, indeed !   But now 'tis time to move
Upon our westward journey with the sun.

ACT III.

SCENE.—A green space surrounded by woods.   A number of
country jakes dancing.   The moonlight falls on the scene.
BLAUVELT—DE PETZY.

DePet.   Cheer up ; this is no time for gloominess.
Go join the dance.
  Blau.   I'm worn and weary, and am sick at heart,
Seeing I've searched to find her that I love
These many days, and have not heard of her.
Oh, Sylvia, thou idol of my heart,
Why didst thou thus escape from me so strangely ?
Was she not sweet ?   Did ever the beauties of earth,
The roses, daises or wild buttercups,
So close their eyes and die so joyfully
That their spirits might go into that heaven
Which is her lovely form ?   Yet now she's lost !
But over the world I'll search,
From icy lands within the bitter north,
Beneath cold skies that are as blue as steel,
Where the limbs freeze and men die piece by piece,

To scorching wastes where burn the sands like fire,
And hot winds parch the throat and dry the tongue ;
Aye, till this frame falls helpless at the last,
Still will I seek her.
    De Pet.   You say you've found
Her father, too, who now lends his assistance
In searching for her.
    Blau.   Aye ; by some marks she showed me on her arm,
It now is proved beyond dispute to us
That this is so ; therefore 'tis harder still
To think of her as wand'ring alone to-night,
While is prepared a happy home for her.
    Jesse.   Come join the dance.   I tak't no compliment
You will not join.   This holding back of yours,
This uncompanionable spirit, will breed
Suspicion of you.   Why, what a long-drawn visage !
You seem infected with a doleful melancholy ;
Your looks, too, tell of sleepless, feverish nights.
This is but wrong.   Cheer up ; 'twill all end well.
The one who makes your face so melancholy
Will yet be kind.
'Tis woman's nature to act opposite
To half her spoken words,
And being a most unreasoning animal,
Say no, when she mean yes.
    Blau.   No woman's words have made me sad to-night,
But other reasons have control of me.
    Jesse.   Ah yes, a woman's reasons still.
Think you, you can deceive a woman thus,
Whose whole discourse is but discourse of love,
From childhood to old age—who acts for love,

Who thinks for love, who speaks for love,
And for her love acts many a mad part—
The center of whose nature's founded on it.
Men you may still deceive, but never a woman,
But reads most clearly signs of love in men.
Did I not hear the tremor in your voice
When first I saw you and you spoke of her?
Have I not seen you wand'ring the fields alone,
Repeating her words as something over-sweet,
Smiling and speaking to yourself alone
Like any madman.   Have I not seen anger
Spring to your eyes when others spoke of her
In other terms than those befitting a goddess—
Their tones too light for your exacting ears?
But I will not torment you with more words,
Seeing you are tormented so by love.

    De Pet.   Where was it that you last lost track of her?

    Blau.   Why, first she wandered through the gloomy
      woods;
Then crossed the fields, and over dusty roads,
Till, reaching the city, she entered into it.
The sounds of city life were strange to her,
And many times did fill here mind with fear;
So I have learned from those who did observe her,
Day in, day out, she wandered through the streets;
Oft run against by hurrying passengers,
And always looking, with anxious, eager eyes,
Upon th' unmindful faces of the crowd,
As if she sought for one she could not find,
At last, 'tis said, she, wearied of this life,
And pined for distant streams, and flowers, and woods.

Now often was she seen beside the ocean,
Listening to read each message that the waves
Had brought from distant ports ;
Or, in the fields
That nearest stood beside the city's edge,
She'd pluck the flowers and gaze upon their faces
As in a mirror, recalling images
Of distant streams, and woods, and mountains blue.
At last those who'd observed lost sight of her,
And from that point I cannot hear of her.

[Enter SYLVIA.]

But who comes here ?   Now, if my eyes deceive me,
And do not bless me, as 'twould seem they do—
What Sylvia, sweet one !   Then we have met at last !

Syl.   At last !   At last !

Blau.   Tell me, where have you been ?
What land has been so lighted by your eyes
There was no need for sun within the day,
Nor stars to shine at night?

Syl.   Three weary days, and nights as weary, too,
I've seen the stars creating light at night,
The mightier sun relieving them by day—
And still have I trudged on most wearily,
Reading the weary hours from shadows at night,
Reading them from the sun's hight in the day,
And yet I found you not.
I grew most weary then ; and while the heavens
Let down a thousand rays of hope to cheer me,
Yet sunk my heart most heavily in me.
But once I saw a light spring from the ground,
Which moved before ; and following after it,

I saw the outline of an angel's hand,
Which held the light until it brought me here.

Blau.   And well might angels help on Sylvia,
Seeing the light that shines from her sweet thoughts
Would make an atmoshpere where they might dwell.
And now the day of parting is o'erpast,
And we will part no more.

Syl.   No more on earth ; and when death comes to one,
Then will we lie, each in the other's arms ;
And when one dies, the other die as well,
And both, still joined, pass to the realms of sleep.

ROMER, KING OF NORWAY.

ROMER, KING OF NORWAY,

A DRAMA.

ACT I.

Scene I.—A room in Welhaven's house.   Hela discovered reading.

Welhav.   What tale is this, my pretty one, that holds
Such full possession over all your thoughts?

Hela.   A pretty tale about two Danish lovers,
But cruel fate between them stood, alas!
For she was cousin to a prince in Denmark,
And he was but commander of his bark;
But in that bark at last he took his love
And dashed out o'er the ocean.

Welhav.   But had the tale a moral?

Hela.   A very pretty moral—they both escaped,
And all their foes were drowned then in the ocean.

Welhav.   Why yes, why yes, but other morals, Hela—

Hela.   Why father, when I read, I read for pleasure
And not for morals.
Morals are plenty over all the earth.
The sweetest one is the night-bird's song :—
The mighty river rolling to the sea
Has a deep moral in its bosom hid.

Welhav.   There are you right,
For pleasure still read on, my pretty one,
And draw while you are young
The honey from this hard, hard earth of ours.

Hela.   Your gloomy tones put evil thoughts in me :—
Has evil news then reached you from the war?

Welhav.   There was a battle, yet still all is well ;
Our king has gained a victory 'gainst the foe—
'Tis whispered that the rebels here in Norway,
Under the lead of that most dang'rous Ehrensvard
Are in a league with this, our Danish foe.

Hela.   He seemed not dangerous, ten years ago,
When he was young and to the world unknown.

Welhav.   But in his heart a hot ambition burned
That had a blaze then dangerous for his country—
I aided him because I knew him poor,
And aided then a viper.

Hela.   Against you too?

Welhav.   He works against my country, and therein
Does work against me.

Hela.   Which way, think you, does his ambition point?

Welhav.   It has no bounds; would leap up to the throne.

Hela.   Nay, but he would not dare to be a king !

Welhav.   But he would dare to play great Cæsar's part; —
And though I serve my king—for 'tis my duty,
I say as all his people oft have said
He is a tyrant, and their love for tyrants
Is like the anger of a tiger ;
And if this outlawed rebel joins with Denmark,
The throne of Norway may be shaken yet.
The priests have made a secret pact with him,

And though it hurts their pride, the noblemen
Join one by one with this bold Ehrensvard ;
But ere he wins there'll be a bloodier war
Than this 'gainst Denmark, each grassy hillock
And every running stream be hued with blood.

Hela. Oh, that men should be of such a nature,
That they can love to slaughter one another ;
To slash and cut and carve the life away ;
To make a hell of pain, a sea of blood,
And then wade through it—oh! 'tis tiger like !—
Were you not old you'd go again to war.

Welhav. My poor, poor Hela ! ill secrets must have out.
The armies of the king have been again
Placed under my command.

Hela. But you"ll not leave me here alone, my father ?

Welhav. Poor daughter, but I must.

Hela. But this is hard,—so very hard indeed—
Go tell the king you're aged and lonely now
And that your daughter has no mother now ;
I know that then his heart will grow as soft
As morning sunlight melting night's dark heart.

Welhav. The king, my child, must have some one to
    lead,—
Poor, pretty Hela, innocent as is
A little bird that flies out o'er the ocean
And learns too soon the tempest and the storm ;
Poor wanderer, it flees so wearily,
And round, and round, and now blown with the gale ;
Now to the north it flies away for help,
Now to the south, then to the west and east,
But none there are to lend a helping hand.

And then at last tired out with battling death,
It shuts its wings, and sinks down 'neath the storm.
    Hela.   Oh, how I shudder thinking of the danger;
The bloody fields, where cannons thunder out,
And from their iron lungs belch clouds of smoke
To veil the horrid scene from heaven's eye,—
I hear the screams, the wails of dying men ;—
See dreadful butchery ; unlimbered cannon,
Dead men and wounded all together lying—
Oh father, father, do not go away !
    Welhav.   Why Hela, child, you make too bloody a scene.
    Hela.   And there are dangers father here at home.
Dangers that now I cannot name to you ;
Oh, stay at home and be here at my side
When I must face them.
    Welhav.   Why, what a little coward now she is.
Enter ROMER.
    Romer.   A merry morning to my pretty cousin.
    Hela.   This is no hour for merriment with me.
    Romer.   The war brings hardships to us all, my cousin,
But we must dare to battle with them too,
And when your father marches 'gainst the foe,
Our palace shall become the while, your home.
    Hela.   A most unhappy home without my father there.
    Romer.   The pleasure at our court will cause you soon
To cast away your grief,
And you may wait upon our suffering queen.
    Welhav.   Cannot the doctors tell then what is wrong ?
    Romer.   They tell me now they fear her mind is mad.
And have commanded that all visitors

Be kept away,
And friends restrained from having converse with her.
   Welhav. Our queen gone mad. Her sweet mind gone.
It seems a wicked thought to dare believe it.
The kingdom of her soul all, all in ruins !
   Romer. The hand of fate ; her father died a madman—
   Welhav. Well I remember when I was a child
I heard my father telling of his madness.
   Romer. Aye, aye, 'tis true—'tis very true indeed.
But now good-by, may you have such success
That glorious honor shall on your gray hairs
Sit as a crown when you return from war.
   Welhav. Nay, I'm too old to love new honors now,
Too old to flattered be, and fooled by them ;
Unless that honor be to serve my king,
Whom not to serve would bring dishonor on me.
               [WELHAVEN and the KING go out.
   Hela. Would that I knew all that's hid in the future !
Oh, that these eyes could look through its dark mist,
And see the secrets that lie hid beyond.
I fear the king ; his actions have a strangeness
When he comes near me, I cannot interpret ;
He gazes, oh, so deeply in my eyes,
As if he sought some far off, hidden thought ;
And yet there is a sadness in his look ;—
But I must now beware of him, for he
Is chilly-hearted, cold, and cruel unless I greatly wrong him.
           Re-enter ROMER.
   Romer. Unless you greatly wrong him.
   Hela. Can you then look upon the closed up mind
And see the swarms of thoughts at work in there?

And do you glance down through the eye, that gate
That opens on the brain.

Romer.   Have charity, my pretty cousin, Hela ;
Why, even I can pity all mankind.

You see we are such poor, weak, villainous wretches; and
we have so many sorrows, and so many pains, Hela, that
we should pity and should love one another.   And there
should be no hate in all the world.   Oh, the little envys and
the little suspicions ; why they are unworthy the heart of a
mouse.   But to have a great heart that beats for all the
world, is worthy of a god.   For you see we are all about
equally good, when you come to think of the trials that
each man is subject to ; and the poor, poor wretch that goes
down, down, until she becomes but a mere shadow of what
she was, may yet have as warm a heart beneath that cold
surface as any of us.   And who knows of the writhings of
heart, and the agony of soul that the poor tender bosom
suffered once, when none would speak kindly, when none
would shed a tear, but all were harsh, harsh, harsh, as the
cruel Winter wind.   Kind?   Why the holy ladies would
pass her by with a look that would harden the heart of an
angel.   My God ! the whole world is upside down.

The terms good and bad, Hela, are human terms, all are
good in the sight of the creator, for he would make nothing
bad.   And who knows but somewhere way up there among
the stars there will be a place that we will pass to, after
going through the gate of death, where we will be all equally well off?   And then we may pass through another gate
of a like death to another world, and so we will go on and
on through the universe like the great stars.

Hela. Forgive me, cousin, I have long been wrong
And in my heart have wrongly slandered you.
   Romer. My gentle cousin, Hela, you're not like all the
    world,
For when we look upon men's petty actions
That are so small, so vilely small,
We soon forget their many nobler deeds,
                    [*it grows gradually darker.*
For look you, Hela, when I wake at night ;
I curse the world to pass away the night—
I think how when two enemies in heart,
With smiles that shadow forth a serpent's venom
Meet on the street.
They're but, my Hela, hideous skeletons,
That clasp their bony hands together.
   Hela. Your mind's a graveyard and there fearful
    horrors
Do buried lie—but I will pity you.
   Romer. You pity me, you gentle hearted one ?—
When all the world besides does hate me now ?
What salve can cure like pity's healing glance ?
When dying men see angels looking down,
Their pitying glances enter in where seas of pains
Are raging wildly and they make a calm.
Ha ! ha, oh, Hela ! Hela ! Hela !
Your sweet eyes, they hold not a curse for me ?
Your rosy lips make not a pretty path,
O'er which hard words come running against me ;—
Methought once that 'twas so.
   Hela. It is not so ; when you have troubles I'll pity you.

Romer. [*Aside.*] Pity? pity? When woman pities, my
   pretty Hela, but one step more and 'tis transformed to
   love.
I thank the heavens that one is kindly left
Of all the wide world that will pity me.
At times I feel so sad, so very sad,
That then I wish my that impatient life
Would break its rein and gallop to the death.
And when I feel so sad, there 's never a one
In all the world that comes to comfort me.
When with each beat my heart does forge a pain
There 's no one then to charm that pain away—
I'm coming, Hela, coming ten days from now,
To take you (as I promised to your father)
To stay within our palace (safe from dangers
That war by chance might bring across your path),
And 'till that time, my time will be employed
In watching how my brainsick wife goes on.
   Hela. Poor gentle woman, but I loved her well.
She loved the world's small winged inhabitants,
And made them her companions oft for hours—
The humming-bird that sent his music waves
To break upon the banks of flowers around ;
The morning lark she loved to listen to,
That charmed the day from out his hiding place—
The swallow, too, that built his hanging house ;—
She loved them all and seemed to be like them
In mind and thought, and in her every action.
What wintry frost could kill so sweet a flower?
   Romer. The chilly breath of madness could alone. [*Exit.*
      [*The moon rises and her light falls through a window.*

Hela. Oh, Ehrensvard; Oh, Ehrensvard, and will I
never see your face again?
Are you too great to think now of your Hela?
Oh, happy hours of childhood passed away
When we were ever near to one another,
When every thought between us two was shared;
When life moved onward like a Summer's dream—
Alas! those hours can never come again,
And I can ne'er again see Ehrensvard.

       [Enter EHRENSVARD through a window.]
And can it be, or do my eyes deceive me?
Oh, Ehrensvard!   [*Falls into his arms.*

  Ehrens. You have not then forgotten me, my darling?

  Hela. Forgotten you? Oh, do not ask me that!
Could I forget you while a thousand dangers
Do ever hem you round? Oh, no, my heart
Is ever trembling when I think of you.
Much rather should I ask, have you not long
Ago forgotten me, while you are led
By fierce ambition.

  Ehrens. All my ambition
Is but to rise up in the world's esteem,
'Till I may claim your hand.
But were my thoughts the very essence—the music
That makes so sweetly sound the voice of reason—
Aye, were my language that a god might use;
Men are not gods to know it, and they will not
For many a century. When I was living
Within your father's house, the king, one day,
Did pass me by, and knowing that I loved you,
Looked on me scornfully, and spoke to me

With scornful words.   And then I took the sword
And waited for my time, which came at last,
And ere that time has grown grey-headed, I
Will write upon his throne the word "destruction."
   Hela.   But you may have to battle 'gainst my father—
   Ehrens.   And if I do, this sword shall ne'er be raised
Against his honored head.
   Hela.   Hark! then I thought
I heard a footstep.   Oh, your life's in danger!
   Ehrens.   Aye, true; 'tis aye in danger.   When I was
    born,
A tempest raged around me on the ocean;
The vessel I was on drove on before it
And crashed upon the rocks that lined the shore.
'Tis strange that only three escaped the wreck,
My mother and my brother and myself;
Some peasants saved us, but I never heard
What did become then of my mother and my brother.
   Hela.   Why, so our king was wrecked one Winter night;
His mother only did escape with him,
And she did have a new-born babe that perished.
   Ehrens..   'Tis strange my greatest enemy should have
A history like my own.
   Hela.   'Tis very strange—
       [*The moon ceases to shine through the window.*
            Enter WELHAVEN.
   Welhav.   Who have we here?
   Ehrens.   One from the rebel, Ehrensvard, who sends
A locket, which your daughter, long ago,
Did give to him.
   Welhav.   Where did you meet the rebel?

Ehrens. Deep in the mountains, and he threatened me
With death if I should not deliver this ;
And he does threaten now that one
Whom he does call no king, but tyrant only.
 Welhav. What learned you there about the rebels move-
  ments ?
 Ehrens I could learn nothing, for 'twas but a moment.
I staid there with them.   [Exit WELHAVEN.
 Hela Thank heaven he's gone !
Oh, my love but you must leave me now ;
I tremble for your life while you are here.
         [Footsteps heard.
Hark ! Hark ! My father comes again.
 Ehrens. Good-by, my darling, when I come again,
I'll bring a thousand keen-edged flashing swords
To ring aloud a melody of death,
And when the glorious sound of victory
Rings to the very vault of yon blue heaven,
Then will I come to find my gentle Hela.
Good-by, one more good-by.   *[Kisses her. Exit.*
   Enter WELHAVEN with soldiers.
 Welhav. Where is your messenger ?
 Hela. Gone.
 Welhav. Why did you let him go ?
 Hela. And did you wish to make the man your captive ?
 Welhav. He was a traitor; in the dark I knew that.

SCENE II. A street.   Enter two Citizens.
 1st Cit. Is this the place ?
 2d Cit. Yes, here they pass at one o'clock to-day ;
They are bold men and they will battle well;

Bold in the heart and cheerful in the mind ;
Such men as they do win great victories.

   1st Cit.   I hear that when the cross roads have been
     reached,
Three thousand Swedish mountaineers will join them.
These men are very bull-dogs for the fight ;
Revelling in blood as 'twere their element ;
They'll charge the foe as to a bloody feast ;
The foe will meet with tigers when they meet them.

Enter 3d Citizen.

   3d Cit.   Our men assemble at the western end ;
Wives cling to their husbands as they say good-bye,
And mothers to their sons are clinging too.

   2d Cit.   It must be sad to see friends forced to part.

   3d Cit.   The word good-bye is drawn from out the mouth
as it were loath to come.   I saw a father in one hand hold
his gun, and in the other, he held his babe, and pressed it
to his bosom ; while to his knees his other children clung,
and begged him not to go away and leave them.

   1st Cit.   'Tis rumored that the king will not lead on
     the army.

   3d Cit.   The rumor shines this time before the truth ;
The King will not lead on against the foe,
He holds not back though from a lack of courage,
For when he battled for his usurped throne—

   1st Cit   Beware what words you speak.

   3d Cit.   Am I a slave to fear a tyrant's power ?
I tell you man before the moon is full
There will be never a tyrant here in Norway.
I say that when the king usurped the throne
More like a tiger than a man he fought,

And with a courage that approached a madness
Did head his armies.
    2d Cit. I have heard it said
That fiends protect him when he faces danger.
And he communes with witches stormy nights
When bleak winds blow along the Norway coasts.
One night, when thunder rattled through the heaven
Before a mountain cavern was he seen.
The lightning showed three witches standing by him,
Whose withered faces shone in its red glare ;
The storm flew past him on the winds cold wings,
And ever and anon the chilly moon
Grinned down between dark clouds.
    1st Cit. Some Laplands saw him too; one Winter right ;
The while the moon held in her yellow arms
Three icy stars up in the chilly heaven,
With spirits dancing on the frozen snow
Beneath the trembling borealis light.
    2d Cit. Who now will head his armies ?
    3d Cit. The General-in-Chief will be Welhaven,
Who has, by reason of his age been long retired.   [*Exit.*
  Enter WELHAVEN dressed as a soldier and HELA with him.
    Welhav. Why now I feel as once I felt of old ;
A soldier's blood is coursing in my veins,
My sinews strain to grasp the sword of battle ;
And now my heart beats marches to that field
Where warlike phantoms flit before my eyes.
Ha ! was the foe even numbered now to millions
We'd raise such flames of battle in their ranks
That rains of twenty Winters could not quench.
    Hela. But father—

Welhav. Ah, Hela, your sweet voice awakes me now—
Like dreams at night, that half dreams only are,
Where we in fancy tread again the past.
A waking thought will ruin all the dream ;
So, your sweet voice, my gentle, lovely one
Has shattered all my vision—
Who'll care for Hela when I'm far away ?
            [*A drum heard in the distance.*
   Hela. Is that the drum that tells us we must part ?
Oh, wretched drum to speak so hideously ?
Your horrid tone does have a blood-like sound ;
Your wretched tone brings shadows to my mind
Of some poor soldier looking up to Heaven,
Yearning for water while he dies of thirst ;
Of some poor soldier wounded cruelly
And breathing out his life in piteous groans—
            [*Soldiers march in.*
   Welhav. Good bye, my child, until we meet again.
   Hela. Oh, but you must not go ! You must not go !
          [Exit WELHAVEN, leading soldiers.

——

ACT II.

SCENE 1.—A room in the Palace. The KING and NIELSEN discovered.

   Romer. Didst ever note the queer twinkle in the queen's
     eye ?
   Niel. Why now I come to think of it my lord, full many
     a time;—most often when she laughs.
   Romer. Aye, aye, of course you have, and do you know
The meaning wrapt up in that act of hers ?

Niel. Why no, I never thought of it in any particular
way, my lord.

Romer. It means that she is mad, mad, Nielsen, mad.

Niel. And now, I come to think of it, I've seen her act
in the strangest ways.

Romer. Aye, aye, and right again ; she's very mad.
Where is she now ?

Niel. She's in her dressing room before her glass.

Romer. A sign that she is mad—
Don't grin, you idiot !

Niel. But my lord, I meant no harm.

Romer. 'Tis very true ;
Simply your idiotic brain did hang
Her idiotic smiles without to dry.
Hang not such filthy garments of your brain,
To flaunt before the sunlight of mine eyes.

Niel. But my lord, I meant no harm.

Romer. Harm, you villain !
Then hold your harmful tongue.
Now tell me man, was't ever in a madhouse ?

Niel. Heaven ! my lord, but you'll not send me to one ?

Romer. Send you to one ! and do you think you are worth
the sending ! Why, when your poor brains once go wool
gathering, we'll cheaply mend them by sinking you, skull,
skeleton, and all,
Down in the belly of the hungry Baltic.
But tell me now, was't ever in a madhouse ?

Niel. Heaven forbid, my lord.

Romer. Or, yet in a charnel house ? where happy worms
make madder merriment.

Niel.   I am slow of thought ; I have been professionally.
Romer.   To the charnel house?
Niel.   To the madhouse, my lord.
Romer.   Villainous people are those same dead men,
and their rotting tongues must needs be long that they
may lie for such a length of time.
And you shall rot ; your bones make odors vile ;
Those eyes of yours grow colorless and dim—
A pleasant time to think on, is 't not so ?
Go kiss your love, and think then with what lips
She will return the action.
Think how a million antic worms one day,
Will build a city in your sweet love's body,
Worms oratorical then in her eyes will preach
A sermon in which there's no hypocrisy ;
Sharp lawyer worms there quarrel for estate—
Lord ! lord! hold your nose man, hold your nose !
                    Enter the QUEEN.
Sweet partner I was telling your physician
About the gate that opens into Heaven,
How angels twang upon their gold harps there,
And devils mock without the crystal walls.
    Queen.   Yes?   And 'tis a sweet tale too ; for oh, it tells
        of rest.
    Romer.   Madam, and which way go you?
    Queen.   Why? to the right.
    Romer.   All thought is left, your mind is not now right.
    Queen.   What is your meaning?
    Romer.   Why at some future date, I'll tell you what I
        mean.   [Exit QUEEN.
Then did you note the wildness in her eyes ?

Niel.   I surely did.

Romer.   And will you swear that surely she is mad ?

Niel.   Why sir—-

Romer.   Why death and blood! you trembling wrinkled
   villian.—

Niel.   Heaven ! my lord, but I will swear it.

Romer.   Did'st ever hear of the seven devils the snake
   begot on Eve's body in Eden ?

And they say gold was a she-devil and the first begotten;—
Go send up Leopold.   [Exit NIELSON.
Oh what a seething cauldron is my soul !
Hell and it's legions do inhabit it,
And drive me on to actions dark as night ;
Dark ! dark ! dark !
The heart is steeled, my strong will torn to tatters
By their vile ravings in this heart of mine !
What demon was it set me on to love ?—
When sun-like love came streaming in my heart,
On what a home did it find waiting there !
The pretty rules of nature turned awry,
All desolation, dark and gloomy there.
Methinks a million fiends still drive me on
To love a woman that I should not love,
And with a love that maddens all within.
I'm in the stream though of my destiny,
Flee then ye spirit of the darkness born,
Bear on my soul through realms of dark despair,
Through hell itself go hold your damned course !
                    [Enter LEOPOLD.]
My queen is mad, hast ever noted it ?

   Leo.   Why no, my lord, I have not noted it.

Romer. Ha! sir, not note it? not note it; you must
have noted it—
Canst comprehend?

Leo. My lord, when I recall to me—

Romer. Your memory wakens then? why very true.
If she grows worse we'll have to take her off—
Canst comprehend? Of course you comprehend—
Aye, and aye, and aye, of course you comprehend.
And they have nice accommodations there—
Oh wretched villain, that I am to think it!
But 'tis a most outrageous world is this—
The seats are softly padded, and the walls—
The queen has fine soft eyes, hast noted it?
Poor mournful eyes, that look so sad at times—
The clanking chains make strangest music there,
And madmen scream out wild accomp'nyments.
Oh, how they howl, and howl like dogs—
And I did dream a dreary dream last night.

Leo. I thought you had no time to dream, my lord,
I heard you walking through the hours of midnight,
Seeming with night to race on to the goal of day.

Romer. A dream? Yet in the passing scenes of night,
I found a place in which to lodge a dream.
I dreamed the world was coming to an end,
And that my heart was filled with thoughts accursed,
And that I dared all hell to punish me.
The sun was dead, and darkness hid the earth,
And death with giant strides tramped o'er the world,
Until it trembled as he strode along.
So thick the darkness as he waded through it,
It eddied 'round him as he moved along.

Full many millions sent up screams and yells,
Of dreadful pains as they lay dying then.
Then all was drowned in sounds of mighty thunder,
That tossed its rattling bolts till heaven shook,
As though 'twould fall in shattered ruins down.
The lightnings flashed and hissed along th' horizon,
And by its light the pale white ocean showed
Foaming and frothing as 'twere mad with fear.
Tossing with its great arms the tiny ships
Against the black and frowning face of heaven ;
A million fiends drag whirlwinds through the air,
And by the lightning's light I saw strange beings,
Some small, some large, some giantlike in bulk,
All come from other worlds to see this earth
Writhing and struggling in her hour of death ;
Here did I wake.

   Leo. My lord, when you were born, even such a storm
Did shake this Norway kingdom. Then it seemed
As though the mighty spirits of that world
That lies beyond the grave were joined in battle.
They cast their thunder crashing through the heaven
'Till earth was shaken to the very centèr,
And all the howling storms raged angrily,
Upon the surface of the foaming deep.
The churches had their steeples swept away ;
Dead men were seen in their grave clothes to rise,
And ghosts were heard through all the night to shriek.

   Romer. And every idiot in this little kingdom
Then thought my birth had brought this fearful storm,
To shadow forth some mighty future woe.
Astrologers, too, gazed upon the night ;—

Up in the corner of the heaven alone,
They found a star whose million rays foretold
A million ills.   And is not this the tale?
   Leo.   It is, my lord—
   Romer.   Oh, wretched fools?
Are these the beings that must dwell with gods?
Go leave me now, for I would be alone.   [Exit LEOPOLD.
This vile suspense must soon come to its end,
Quickly, and quickly, while the moments speed ;—
It matters not if we are parted now,
A little pang upon the parting time,
It dies away, the wounds soon healed again.
All pain is soon forgotten, and all sorrow
Does take time's hand and hurries to the past,
Where soon 'tis buried in a dark oblivion—
             [Enter QUEEN]
Madam I am not worthy of your love,
You are an angel, and a villain I.
Some day your spirit like a rocket shot,
Will pass up through the darkened shade of death ;—
I'll kiss my hand to you and step below,
Where people gnash and cut their teeth anew,
Tear out their eyes and spit upon them there,
Scream, yell, and curse ; tear up the rooted hair,
And make long journeys on a groaning treadmill ;
Considering madam then our after paths,
'Tis best we be divorced.
   Queen.   Oh, there must be a madness in your heart !
Oh cruel ! cruel ! harsh and cruel word !
   Romer.   Look ! Look madam, dost see them !
   Queen.   What my lord ?

Romer. Why fiends, madam, fiends; see how their horrid eyes gaze down on me. Spirits of darkness stand back! Stand back! My time is not yet come.

Queen. I see nothing, my lord ;—where are they?

Romer. Have you eyes and see them not? They are all around us, and they reach out to seize my soul. [*Strikes in the air with his dagger.*] Back, stand back! I fear you not! Nor earth, nor heaven, nor hell!

Queen. What is 't, my lord?

Romer. Fiends, spirits and devils, madam! See how they surround me! And see the ghastly gaze within their eyes— Ha! they are gone.

Queen. Heaven, how the sweat rolls from your brow.

Romer. They come from hell, to hell they have returned.

Queen. And hell in you does counsel this divorce--

Romer. 'Tis heaven has done it, and it must be so.

Queen. Oh cruel! cruel! harsh and cruel words.

Romer. Aye madam, yes: my words, each in their hands
Hold thoughts brimful of direst cruelty ;
My wicked acts might loom up mountains high
Above those deeds 'tis said the devils act.
Thinking of all those dead things we were once ;
How once I loved your outward form and feature,
Till the reaction blighting all that had been,
Did cast a sallow, foul and sickly hue
Over all nature.—Do you remember,
How once I said the flowers crushed by your feet
Would still rise up and then gaze after you
With sweet forgiving looks.
Oh, I am sick! What hypocrites we are ;
And things inanimate are false, and lie to us :—

But in this, my career, I'm driven onward
And am not led by any will of mine.
I long have striven against an inclination,
That in my brain sits there a monarch
And rules my other thoughts.

    Queen.   And I ; have you no thought, not one, for me ;
Because you have this foolish fantasy,
This childish thought, am I to be deserted,
Be left behind abandoned to those waves
That from the sea of life will surge and break
With sullen roar above the heads of those
Who've sunken downward drowned beneath its depths.

    Romer.   It cannot be in any otherwise,
My mind 's now firmly fixed in this resolve
That we must part.

    Queen.   And you've no reason yet to give for this ;
    Romer.   My reason lies in this, that it must be.
    Queen.   Your reason lies in this, that in your heart
There's not a spark, an idea, no sensation
To show you up a man ; but in that heart
Is cruelty and cunning intermixed ;
And there they hold such sway that gentler thoughts
Have long ago fled from the hideous scene.

    Romer.   Now I have a reason
Which ne'er before had I to urge against you.

    Queen.   If reasons were the weapons that you used
In this harsh war against me,
Why, I would bring a million reasons,
With such a bristling front
That then yours would not dare to battle with them.
To gain your purpose you would break God's laws,

And love another, though you 're bound to me.
That cruel love of yours which once was mine,
Doth like some vine, whose roots are in the grave,
Grow to another.
    Romer.   All of those possessions
Which ever were, and more than all before
Shall still be yours.
    Queen.   Nay, strive to speak your harshest words to me,
The harshest words that ever cursed a language
Were sweet besides these hideous promises.
The grave would soon seem like a gentle home,
For which my thoughts would never cease to long,
Lived I in that which you would picture to me.
    Romer.   And yet it still must be, and we must part.
    Queen.   A year ago had I been told 't was so
I would have spurned the thought
That in humanity could be such coldness.
    Romer.   Yet, I will still be ever kind to you ;
And all you wish—that all shall still be yours.
    Queen.   And if your kindness took this fearful form
My misery then would tear from out my brain
Each record of the past ; each gentle story
Of days gone by ;
And in my brain, that had become a ruin,
Would thoughts of madness come to hide themselves.
    Romer.   My life was all laid down, in all its course
Before I drew my breath ; and I have learned
From those that speak to and can hear the tones
Of them that answer from beyond the grave,
That henceforth we must part.
    Queen.   I scarce can trust you in this fearful change.

This seems no vision of the day, but one of the night,
A monstrous birth brought from some dream at midnight,
And if you do not change your mind in this,
I call on heaven to crush your cruel schemes ;
And heaven will lend me aid, for even now
Your subjects fast grow secretly your foes ;
They call you now a tyrant,
And while they point to many a headless corpse ;
They work for their revenge—

    Romer. Then you have turned your face against me too,
Ha ! Madam, is it so? Then is it so ?
Why, Madam, you are mad.
            [*The xueen is standing by a canary bird's cage.*
    Queen. [*speaking to the bird.*] Did your strong mate
    then call your little brain
A mad brain, too, and lock you in this cage ?
Or have you done some fearful villainy
That men should lock you in this pris'ner's cell ?
Poor prisoner? What horrid crime indeed
Did you have malice in your heart to do ?
And were there none to hear you sweetly rave ;
Not one to listen to your poor complaint ;
Nay, nay, they passed you by. Hey, was't not so ;
When men had dragged you from your little home,
Then did your friends come trooping on behind
To grin and gape and stare at your despair—
With wisest faces then did they remark,
That they had ever noted your black heart—
Your villains face ? ha ! ha ! And here you've been
Hopping about—singing for many a year,
Pouring your sorrows on the dumb, cold air—

Romer.   Such is her madness, as it ever was.

Queen.   Oh, call this but some cruel jest of yours
And I will suffer all, that you may laugh.

Romer.   See you how sharp and cunning now she is.

1st Off.   A sign she's mad; her madness gives her cunning.

Queen.   Then is it so? My lord, can you be kind?
I ever loved you well; and will you now
So roughly spurn that love? Oh, do not thus!
I'd rather die than you should use me so—

Romer.   Grasp hold of her, for she will rave forever.

Queen.   Oh, wait one moment for kind heaven's sake?
A little moment, ages now to me;
Oh, let me flee far to some darkened forest
That I may tell the silence there my sorrows.
Oh, anything but this most dreadful fate,
For Christ's sake do not act so cruelly!
Go see the sun and note how kindly, gently
He lays his ray upon the rose's breast;
The day with twilight smoothes the path for night;
The night with dawn prepares the way for day;
The passing hours relieve each other on
The march that leads down to eternity—
Oh, be not thou more cruel than all these.

Romer.   I will not be
More cruel that your hours
That move so silently;
This deed shall be as silently forgot;
And like the people on this earth of ours
I'll take your rose to cover up the deed,
For roses oft do grow o'er skeletons—
Now lead her out.

Queen.   Oh, hold ! Oh, hold ! For sweet heaven's sake.
My lord, oh kill me, rather than do this
Here is my bosom if you have a dagger,
Here is my bosom bare and white as snow ;
Now dip a dagger in my heart's warm blood,
And write in bloody letters on my bosom
A host of curses 'gainst my poor dead body.
   Romer.   It shows me foolish that I let your madness
Still strive to reach my pity.
   Queen.   What can I say ? all thoughts desert me now,
And will not come to help me in this time—
In this hard moment that is filled with horrors.
My very blood does freeze to think of it,—
A madman's cell—a madman's cell my home ?
Oh, that I had a mighty giant's mind,
And in my mouth a tongue so sad and mournful
That heaven's winds would cease to moan and listen ;
And all the clouds would come to hear me speak ;
Then would I speak until the hard stones wept,
And streams were silvering every mountain side
The whole world over !
Then would I come to plead, my lord, with you—
   1st. Off.   She we seize her, my lord ?
   Queen.   But this is cruel, this is very cruel !
Oh, that the angels coming from high heaven
Would drop their tears while passing on your heart,
Or, send their whispers floating over it,
To drive away the ghoul like anger there,
   Romer.   Go, lead her out—
   Queen.   The devil himself methinks might pity me.
But you will not—

Romer.   Go, lead her out.

                    [Exit OFFICERS with the QUEEN.

This love for Hela's fiendish, hellish, outrageous;
It is a smoke the winds have blown from hell.
Yet, am I dragged on as one in a dream.
Divorce comes next; we'll have a holy Bishop
To pass that sentence through his loving heart—
God! God! What villians we are!
Still on, and on, must run my mad career,
Upon the rushing stream of destiny.
Hark to the music that accompanies me!
A million devils that dwell in the air,—
I see them ever crowding 'round my path.
I see them in the darkened hour of night
Come vaulting o'er the rolling clouds of night;
I see them racing with the hurricane,
And ever grinning as they race along.
Aye, grin and grin; let hell lurk in each grin;
And shoot your hellish eyes like darts of fire.
I'd dare ye to th' encounter wer't upon
The brink of that great pit, where flames flash up,
And lick their tongues against the face of heaven.

ACT III.

SCENE.   A hall in which a number of Norwegian Noblemen and
Bishops are assembled.   ARVICKA, one of the Noblemen, presiding.

Arv. [*Rising.*] We're gathered here upon affairs so grave,
That all the heart of Norway, now does throb
In their regard.   A matter 'tis to make
The spirits of your fathers, in their graves
Wake from their gloomy sleep, to come again

In creaking armor, and with rusty swords ;
To teach their sons to rise 'gainst tyranny.
Th' unworthy head of Norway.
Forgetting law would make his people slaves ;
I am a slave, and you ;—we all are slaves ;
I speak it calmly, do you hear my words ?
Slaves, Norwegians ! Slaves ! Ha ! Is 't an honor
That you do meekly listen to the sound !
Is all the fire that burned your fathers hearts
Wrapt with them in their shrouds.   If this be so
Better our county sank beneath the ocean ;
Better the storms did roar above our heads
And the white billows, white as sepulchres—
But I forget, the age has passed beyond me,
And I am stranded on a shoal of time,
Where men had rather died than serve a tyrant.

   1st Nob.   The burden's on us, and we groan beneath it
But quickly will we cast that burden down
When some bold leader rises up to guide us.

   1st Bish.   And if we have no leader, then will we
Rush all together 'gainst our tyrant king
And in the shock receive our death or freedom.

   Arv.   Ha ! I have wronged you
For now I see that those poor words I speak
Have waked the sleeping tiger in each breast
And every noble eye now fiercely gleams
With lightening that does go before the storm.
So had these thoughts stirred up your fathers breasts
'Till they, with firm clenched hands, had torn the heart
From him who robbed them of their liberty

My heart grows warm to look upon you now,
While such men live, all tyranny must die.

2d Nob. Show us the way that freedom may be found,
And we will seek wer't through the halls of death.

3d Nob. Strong is the reason that does urge me on
To rise up in rebellion 'gainst the king;
I had an aged father that this tyrant
Did load with chains, and cast into a dungeon,
Where all was chilly, dark and desolate;
And here his chains did hold him many a year
Waiting in patience 'till his end might come.
The end did come, for when one Winter night
The midnight hours on tiptoe hurried by,
I stood beside him while he fell asleep
To sleep that sleep that freed him from his chains;
Soon then the sun did break night's barriers down
And all his flood of light came flowing in
That showed his poor dead face that had a smile upon it,
A sweet sad smile, a very pretty smile,
Like sunlight, and his face a Summer's morn;
A smile that seemed to laugh at tyranny.

2d Nob. I had a son that carried all my hope;
A son that I had watched through many a year.
As he grew up from childhood's years to youth,
From youth to manhood; and then at that time
When all the greater dangers of his life
Had been passed by, this king did hew him down,
And left his body i' the sun to rot
Where dogs might feed upon it.

Arv. A record this to make the king of darkness
Grow pale with envy; do you hear, my lords,

The noble record of your noble king ?
Methinks that now you do not need a drum
To stir your spirits.
    1st Bish. And we would add grave charges to these
        charges ;—
As you condemn him in this earthly world,
So we condemn him in the world to come ;
There shall he burn in fire unquenchable,
Where he shall yearn for but a drop of water which angels
shall deny him. For he has robbed the church of all those
lands which heaven has provided.
    2d Bish. Is this a king to sit on Norway's throne ? A
king who robs the holy mother church of all her lands ? A
king who scorns the cross ?
Heaven's curse will be upon the land he governs.
    Arv. These charges, did they bear far lesser weight,
Would paint him for so black a hearted villain,
That were he cast from off some jutting rock
Headlong into the frothing surf below,
Or carried down into the roaring Maelstrom,
The punishment would be by far too light.
    2d Nob. If at some time when Denmark sends his ships
Loaded with warriors that against our king
Are sent to battle, we joined with Ehrensvard,
The foreign foe would then become our aid,
And then might we rise up against our king.
    3d Nob. 'Tis said that thousands flock to Ehrensvard,
And in the mountains join his wandering bands.
But in those mountains he is barriered now,
For all the warriors that the king can spare
From those he sends to battle with this Denmark,

He sends 'gainst him.   But knowing every stronghold
Deep in the mountains Ehrensvard does hide,
And in the night-time steals upon his foe,
Or comes upon them when they're off their guard,
Then swiftly leads his men back to their stronghold.
   2d Nob.   'Tis rumored now the Danes prepare a fleet
To send against us.
   Arv.   Then let us dethrone
This king and tyrant.   Then will we o'ercome
With ease this Denmark, and will send his fleet
To find the bottom of the Baltic sea.
But if the deed is done there's no to-morrow
Must wait its doing.   Now the time is hot ;
The people now do hate the king that rules them,
And now does hostile Denmark come against us.—
'Tis in the rush and whirlwind of the time
That noble deeds are done ; so let this deed
Be now done.
   1st Bish.   But is Ehrensvard now ready ?
   Arv.   He only waits for us to join him.
   2d Bish.   Have you then heard from him ?
   Arv.   Last night he came to me.
   3d Nob.   Ev'n like a spirit from the world of death
He's everywhere, and I have heard it said
That once he went disguised before the king.
   Arv.   If he had but been born to be a monarch,
He'd make the world his kingdom.
   1st Bish.   Let him then
Become a monarch and rule over Norway.
   Arv.   Stout hearts must let him and sharp blades of steel;
They that would let him must have on their side,

The hours of midnight when the lazy moon
Looks sadly down upon the quiet world ;
When sleep does hold the world in chains of silence.
Then they, would let him,
Must slip out 'neath the mantle of the night
And steal on towards the palace of the king,—
And one must reach the bedroom of the king;
If it proves that one cannot reach the room,
Then all must strive, though o'er a bloody path,
To reach it.

  3d Bish. The palace though is strongly guarded.
  Arv. There are a thousand ways to make a strong guard
   weak.
All here are friends to me, and friends to Norway,
I fear not then to give this secret to you,—
That Ehrensvard will be this night with us,
To share the deed.

  2d Bish. Is it not though too soon ?
  Arv. My lord if 'tis too soon,
There'll be no time when 'twill be late enough.
To-night at twelve,
When does the bell up in the palace tower
Toll with its mournful note the hour of midnight,
Let every man come armed into the grove,
That's to the eastward of the palace wall.
Then when the sentinels on the wall are changed
We'll make our entrance through the eastern gate.

    Enter a messenger
  Mess. My lords, the king does send his greeting to you
And says that he is coming to preside
Here at your meeting.   [*Exit messenger.*

1st Bish. Then we all are lost.

2d Bish. Oh why was I enticed to turn against him?
Woe, was the day when 'gainst the lords anointed
I turned this face of mine.

3d Bish. I too have erred
But all the while my heart did rightly beat,
The flesh alone was weak.

4th Nob. We're all lost men.

Arv. What, can a moment change men's natures so?
Methought three valiant bishops were here with me,
Whose indignation burned against their ruler?
Truly the flesh is weak—The flesh turns traitor—
It matters not,
For soon the king will cast the traitors' flesh
In some dark dungeon; or perchance the head
Will by an ax be severed from the flesh.

4th Nob. And do you think the king does know already
Why we have met?

Arv. Surely he does,
And I doubt not that in his punishment
He'll be severity turned tiger-like.
Our only hope is now to stand together,
And when he enters pierce him to the heart;
'Tis no time now to act the woman's part,
Our hope, our life depends upon our action.

2d Bish. But if we fail?

Arv. The failure will be glorious; for then the sound
of this glorious deed shall be born by the billows of the
ocean of time and cast up on the shores of eternity.
Prepare then now to act a noble part
Or die a noble death.   [*A trumpet sounds in the distance.*

1st Bish.   The king approaches ! Oh ! our fate is sealed.

4th Nob.   Our only hope is now to kneel before him,
And pray of him a pardon for our treason.

2d Nob.   Our only hope.

Arv.   You too, my lord ? Oh heaven !
My heart grows sick.   Are these my countrymen ?
God help my country !
Are these the men whose eyes did seem to blaze
With fire that flashed as from the tiger's eye,
Whose sinews strained at but the thought of danger ?
Methinks that if your fathers now are 'round you
Their pale eyes weep to look upon their sons.
Is there not here one patriotic hand
Will lift a dagger 'gainst the tyrant's bosom ?
What, never an answer ? Truly then you're doomed.

                               [*Trumpet sound snear.*

2d Bish.   Our fate will soon be known.

Arv.   Our only hope is in his death.
Once more I ask are there none here to aid me ?
What, none ?
Then will I leave you to await your doom—

1st Bish.   Come let us go to meet him,
And throw ourselves before him.

Arv.   [*Springs to the door and draws his sword.*]
Make but th' attempt, and I will cut your bodies
Into a thousand parts.
Oh, that my Countrymen should be so base—
[*The door is forced open by soldiers from without. Arvicka is seized after much resistance; and the others submit without resistance. The king takes his seat in the chair of state.*]

Romer.   My noble lords continue with this business ;
Cast out the music of your eloquence
In golden notes to tremble on the air ;
Now imitate the dead Demosthenes,
And make dead Cicero, to shake his bones
In ghastly envy.   Where are your tongues my lords
Are they then in the grave with Cicero :
Why have you met together ? Ha ! Bishops here ?
Surely some deed of heavenly character ;
A heavenly light does fill your holy eyes—
Why are you here ?
  1st Bish.   We do not know, my lord.
  Romer.   You're right, my lord ; for man does nothing
    know ;
We're built of dust and our thoughts are dust, and the dust
knows nothing.   Our thoughts are built from what we see
around us, and that is dust.   The heaven man dreams of—
'tis earth and dust, vile rotting dust.
Hark you ! what shall we call the man—
You know what I would say—
  1st Bish.   My lord a poor, poor wretch who grievously
    has erred.
  Romer.   Who grievously has erred.   Is he a villain ?
  1st Bish.   My lord, I fear it.
  Romer.   [*to Arvicka.*] And you, my lord ?
  Arv.   And if you were that king,
That man would be a noble patriot,
Who saw no danger in a tyrant's frown,
But only saw his country drifting on
To crash upon the rockbound shore of ruin ;
Who heard alone the cries of agony ;

A million voices mingled with the storm,
That drove his country onward to destruction.
    Romer.   And is your hate against me then so strong?
    Arv. My lord, I hate you not.   If I did hate you
I were unworthy then to do this deed.
    Romer.   And for th' attempt to do this noble deed
You now shall die, and sleep down in the ground,
Where slimy waters shall ooze through your bones ;
Your jaws shall gape, and grin a ghastly grin,
Your eyes shall stare as they did ne'er before,
And then we'll have a stone above your head
For crows to light upon, and make you famous.
    Arv.   I fear not death ;
'Tis but a step from daylight to the dark ;
'Tis but a night that comes before the time,
Then like a man I dare to face that night.
The world is change ;—the universe is change,
Then when my sun sinks down into the night
Must I too change.
    Romer.   Bring in the headsmans' axe,   [*Exit a soldier.*
We'll give the worms a banquet.
My holy bishops, soon th' unholy earth
Will fade away before your holy eyes,
And the great death will ope his ebon gates,
And lead you through into his midnight kingdom;
And when you pass into his mighty kingdom
Where all is ruin, and where all is black,
Then will you learn if two and two are four—
There's naught that can be known 'till after death.
My lord, I envy you, for you will learn
What man can never know.   What is't to live,

To sleep, to eat, to walk upon the street,
Why rats, why vermin do they not the same?—
To bow, to grin, to gape at one another,
And then some pestilence,
Does blow away the little flames of life—
To die and sleep the dark and gloomy sleep,
And then?

    2d Bish. My lord, we cast ourselves before you here——

    Romer. What, do you fear to die? You who so oft
Have thundered gainst the flesh,
This wretched flesh, vile and abominable—
Prepare yourselves to die.   *[Enter a soldier with an axe.*
                         [The king takes it and feels the edge.
That this should have the power to make an end
Of all that's mortal in this being man——
My lord, Arvicka, you are now released,

    Arv. What, now released!

    Romer. I said released, but if you rise again
In arms against me, then your life shall end.
Beware, I say, beware then my revenge.
Now chain these coward bishops hand to hand
And 'till our further orders cast them in a dungeon.

           Enter a messenger hurriedly.

    Mess. My lord! The Danes gave battle to the army
That headed was by the aged Welhaven,
And they defeated him and took him prisoner.

ACT IV.

Scene 1. A room in the Palace. The moon shines through a window. Hela discovered by the window.

Hela. The time flies on ; a stream of strange events
Into the ocean of the past does swiftly flow.
The time flies on, upon the wings of madness ;
The years roll by like heavy darkened clouds,
That drive before the gale ; and Summer comes
Upon the heels of Winter, which follows on again.

Enter King.

Romer. What, Hela, alone ! Here all alone to-night ?
What thoughts are yours that move in unison
With that same stealthy tread with which night glides
        along.
To steal our lives away !

Hela. My thoughts were even about this life of ours,
And I was thinking how strange a dream it is.

Romer. 'Tis a queer dream, Hela, a queer, queer dream.
And why we are born at all to dance this mad dance across
the stage of life, is the most wonderful part of it. And
when we're here what more do we than to mimic the actions
of the worms of the dust ? We build up cities that they
may fall down again, we raise up empires, and the empires
decay ; children are born to us and they slaughter one another,
and still the same act is reacted, and yet acted again, 'till one
grows sick in the contemplation of it.

Hela. But every one of these beings has a hope of
heaven, and that makes them noble. And look at the ambition that burns in the human heart ; is it not worthy of
a God ? All men look forward to the accomplishment of
some great deed before they die.

Romer. And it is never accomplished.
The only pleasures in th' acccomplishment,
When the deed 's done, 'tis nothing.
But let us drop the gloomy thought of life ;—
See how the moonlight's trembling silver flood
Does pour a-down 'yond whitened age'd cliffs.
  Hela. To-night the moon looks pale and melancholy,
To these, my eyes, perhaps because my heart
Has all the day been sad. -
  Romer. You, Hela, sad ?
I thought that all the sadness of the world
Was in my heart. And why then are you sad ?
  Hela. I have been thinking of my age'd father,
How he is chained down in some gloomy dungeon,
Within the Danish kingdom—
  Romer. Aye, Hela, but we'll set your father free ;
This very night at midnight will I lead
My army on in person 'gainst the foe.
  Hela. What, will you lead them ?
  Romer. Yes, have you not seen
Through all the day the soldiers in the streets?
  Hela. And why do you start in the night?
  Romer. In time of war one hour is like another.
When there is danger from a foreign foe
We will not sleep 'till that time he is conquered.
  Hela. Some say the reason that you have for hurrying,
Is that you would give battle to the foe
Before your soldiers, that are mutinous
Rise up against you.
  Romer. Who was the traitor
That dared to utter such lying words as these ?

Hela.   I do not now remember.
Romer.   And if you did
His head should rot upon our battlements.
    Hela.   'Twill be a cold, cold march ; the snow is on the
      ground.
    Romer.   The soldiers will be warm upon the march.
But Hela, oh ! My heart will then be cold,
Colder than is the snow upon the ground,
For all my brain is racked with madden love,
A love for which I've given my all in life,
A love will kill my soul when I am dead ;
A blazing love that burns my heart to ashes,
Dost hear me !
Ha !   Fiends of hell, why do you gaze on me ;
In love, sweet Hela, in love.
    Hela.   Who do you love ?
    Romer.   Who do I love ?   Then thou'lt be like the moon.
That has been cold as ice for many a year,
And ever has played distant to the sun,
That has so long with love been burning for her.
Whom do I love ? why I do love that one
For whom I have been dying many year.
    Hela.   Whom do you love ?
    Romer.   I love you, Hela, and with a love so strong,
That death alone can melt it from my heart ;
'Tis with an iron love.
    Hela.   What, are you mad ?
    Romer.   What, am I mad ? Ha ! I am mad, my darling.
Mad, mad, mad for your love !   But I have crushed it
Down, down, down within my heart;
Though death were in its breath,

I'd rather battle with the midnight storm,
Than with this love ;—than crush this love
I'd rather strive to drive the Maelstrom back.
I'd rather hope to conquer death's dark kingdom,
Than strive against the whirlwind of my love.
   Hela. It cannot be.
   Romer. It cannot be !
And is't for this I've sold my soul to hell ?
Have fought with spirits through the hours of midnight ;—
With devils that did gaze down through the darkness ;
That sought to take my soul before the time,
And drag it down in chains to blazing hell.
   Hela. Yet I did never tell you that I loved you.
   Romer. In words you did not, but your eyes did speak.
Perhaps 'twas but an action as a woman
Whose dev'lish nature ne'er can be subdued;
Hell's counterpart in a woman's heart,
Though she seems pure as is the evening star.
Your eyes did speak a vile hypocrisy
And like two fiends did tempt me on and on.
   Hela. And after all then you do love me not ?
   Romer. Since first the world did dash out on its course,
All freighted with its madmen,
No man did ever love a woman yet
As I have loved you.
   Hela. Then cease you now to love,
For I can never give my love to you.
   Romer. [*Grasps her by the arm.*] Hark ! will you crush
     me.
And can those eyes that never a star in heaven
Can mock in brightness, now look sternly on me ;

And you'll not love me ; will not love me Hela ?
Oh, God !

    Hela.   There is another that I love, my lord.

    Romer.   Harsh ! harsh ! harsh ! are your words.
Now time rush on and cast your hours away,
And make each yesterday a blank, a nothing.
Let every hour have now a poisonous breath,
To put this angry life of mine to sleep.
Oh death, sweet balm to all man's earthly woes,
The mighty night where all his pain does sleep ;
Grand terminus to all the ills of life,
Come o'er me now.

    Hela.   Speak not so gloomily.

    Romer.   Are you my friend ? I never had a friend,—
Let me gaze in those eyes.   They melt my soul,
Take them away.   And will not, cannot love me--
Ah ! You are like the rest.   Your soul 's a sepulcher.

    Hela.   Oh, speak no more, in human kindness speak not.

    Romer.   You do not love me, and my life has been
Cold, cold, cold ; but like a warrior,
My heart has battled 'gainst the ills of life ;
My life has been Sahara's desert lined
With whitened skeletons of hopes all dead ;
But now all's down, my weary heart is broke.

        [IDUNA, the queen, sings within.]

       The night came on, the wild wind roared,
          My sweet love went to sea ;
       But the greedy sharks, they ate up him
          And he never came back to me.

    Romer.   'Tis the mad queen.

Enter QUEEN.

Queen. Are you the king of Norway ? Then I will ask you to command the winds to cease howling up in my room, for they keep me awake o'nights.

Hela. Poor lady, poor lady !

Queen. Yes, I am a poor lady, I'm a very poor lady, and I live all alone in my room ; and no one comes to visit me there for they say it is dangerous. Shall I sing you a song ?

[*Sings*]   Hey, pretty bird, pretty bird.
　　　　　　Sing me a song.
　　　　　　Hey, pretty bird, pretty bird,
　　　　　　　　Hey, oh !

Hist, sir, don't tell anybody, but I gave all I had in the whole wide world, don't you know ; way back there ; way back in the past ; way back, it hurts my eyes to look so far back ; way back there I gave everything I had for that song. Don't tell anybody now don't tell a word—

Romer. Mad now, indeed—

Queen. Don't tell anybody for all the world ; not for all the world ; for then somebody might hear about it, and it would hurt their feelings, and that's something that I never would do, for you see that I'm a woman, and no, I never would do that.

Hela. My poor, poor lady ; better were she dead.

Romer. Her brain is dead now, dried up, vanished.

Queen. Yes, her brain is dead, dried up, vanished. Ha ! Ha ! 'Tis very funny, is it not ? Why very, very funny. [*To king*] You are a humorous man ; a very funny man, and you make me laugh [*throws herself in his arms*], and I do love you with an iron love !

SCENE II.—A street. A number of citizens discovered.

1st Cit. We'll have a king now will rule us as a king. King Romer was too hard on the poor people, and gave all to the nobles.

2d Cit. Yes, and I'll stand by you there, for there has been more hanging done in his reign than was ever done before.

3d Cit. True, true, for I had two friends hung last Summer; as honest men as ever drew breath.

2d Cit. And he was great for making new laws, which oppressed the poor. For he made laws against this, and laws against that, so that there was hardly anything a man could do out of the ordained way, without being taken to law for it.

1st Cit. Aye, what with having his Senate pass this, and his Senate pass that, and then repealing it all again, we've got so many laws that it's not safe for an honest man to live in the country. But we'll have Ehrensvard now, and he'll be a king to beat all the kings that ever went before him.

3d Cit. Aye, aye, the poor man now will be able to look the rich man in the eyes, and talk as bold to him as the best of them.

5th Cit. At any rate we'll have a new deal all 'round.

Enter NIELSON and LEOPOLD.

Leo. Ha! my noble hearted men do you wait the approach of the new king? He is to enter at the western gate, to pass along this street, and to enter the palace. The street is to be hung with flags, and the people will greet him with waving handkerchiefs; flowers will be cast in his path, as he rides along on his black war horse. When he enters the city gate the bells will ring out such a sound that the wind will perchance bear it as far as the battle-field where the tyrant fights.

Niel. And to-night the heavens will be aflame with fire-works.

2d Cit. We'll have a great king now to rule us.

Leo. The old king cannot be spoken of in the same breath with him. You all know how he oppressed the church and the nobles—

Cits. No, no, no!

1st Cit. The poor; 'twas the poor that he oppressed.

Leo. And did I not say he oppressed the poor?

2d Cit. You said the nobles.

Leo. Aye, and did he not oppress the nobles?
And the poor more than the nobles.

Niel. But the time approaches for the arrival of the new king. Then go swell the crowd that is to meet him.

[Exit citizens.

Leo. The die is cast for us, but in the venture,
There'll be success. For now will this new king
Be firmly seated on his new-found throne.
With but one voice the people all do shout;
The air is burdened with the sound of praise
They give the king.

Niel. But every voice shouts with a selfish end;
And should the old king be a conqueror
And drive the Danes back to their ships again,
Then will they shout in voices just as loud
In praise of him. We have abandoned him
From selfish motives, so the people do.
Our deeds that are called pure and charitable
Are at the bottom done in selfishness;

Our love is selfish, and our lives are so,
'Tis selfishness that runs this might world.

Enter a Citizen.

Cit.   The Senate has gone forth to meet the king,
Or he that will ere sun-down be the king.
The clergy go out first, and then the Senate;
Next come the lawyers and the learned men,
And last of all the people crowd behind.

Niel.   The people crowd behind ;—
What a strange silence dwells within the air,
The city seems as still as death to-day.

Cit.   'Tis fitting that there should be such a silence
Before the glorious sound to soon break forth.   [*Exeunt.*

SCENE III.—The Senate.   EHRENSVARD seated on a throne.   The nobles and people assembled.

Arv.   Long has our country borne a heavy yoke;
That yoke is cast aside.   Who once did live
Beneath the shadow of a threatening sword
No longer fear; for they are freemen now.
Freedom now fills this Norway air with sweetness;
Who once did hold their lives but by a thread,
Will think of tyranny but as a dream.
Trade will survive; our land become a garden;
And when again there's peace in all the land,
Our country then will rise up like a giant,
And shake away the deadning sluggishness,
With which the evil government before
Had cast around it.
Trade breathe the breath of life, the arts be introduced,
Schools will be founded and great colleges,
Our country shall become as great as any

In all the world.   Who helped us to secure
This glorious freedom for the land we love,
Who suffered long to gain our liberty,
Who battled long to break the tyrant's chain,
Deserves to be the ruler of the land ;
And I, because the people all have urged me,
With a glad heart deliver in their name,
This crown, the symbol of their liberties.
                              [Presents a crown to EHRENSVARD.
 Nobs.   Hail to the new king of Norway !
 Arv.   And let me be the first to kneel before my king.
                              [*People shout within.*
 Ehrens.   Rise, noble man; hadst thou been made the king,
A worthier man had then been made the king ;
For I am but a rough time-hardened soldier,
Unused to ruling in a time of peace ;
And only know to lead an army on,
Of marches, countermarches, strategy ;
Or lead them through a swollen torrent,
Or 'cross ravines ; to make concealed marches,
But thou wast born and bred to rule a land,—
But yet if I, of all the most unworthy,
Am chosen by the people for their ruler,
I'll do my best to serve them.   [*Bells ring within.*
    2d Nob.   Hark to the sound !   the bells cast forth sweet
         music,
To tell the people they have now a king,
To make their land become a glorious land.
  Ehrens.   Now, first of all, my lords, we must prepare
To overthrow the former tyrant king,
If he should not by Denmark be o'erthrown.

His forces are encamped upon a mountain,
And in the valley is the Danish army ;
If, when his army meets the Danes in battle,
They conquer him ; our throne becomes secured ;
But if he wins the battle, then must we
O'ercome the victor.

Arv.   There is naught to fear,
The people all would give their lives for you,
And think it then a glorious privilege
That they might die, while battling for their land.

Ehrens.   Repair we now, my lords, until the night,
When we will have a banquet spread in honor
Of this, our grand occasion.

SCENE IV.—A room in the Palace.   EHRENSVARD and HELA.

Ehrens.   'Tis reached at last ;—the top of my ambition,
For many a year I've struggled on and on,
Through disappointments that did chill the heart,
For many a year have struggled when even hope,
Did almost leave me; but a memory still,
Of words of scorn that once were spoken to me
Did urge me on to crush the one that scorned me.
Unknown, and poor, a king one time did scorn me,
And laughed at me because I loved you, Hela;
But now I scorn the king.   Canst thou remember,
When we were children, and did play together ?

Hela.   The memory of that time can never leave me ;
That time seemed brighter than the earth seems now,
The flowers seemed sweeter, and the song of birds
Was music that has ne'er been heard again.

Ehrens.   Do you recall how on the ocean's beach
We wandered hand in hand for many a mile,

Climbing around the rugged jutting rocks,
And listened to the music of the sea
That casts its mighty waves against the rocks,
To fall back frothing in their fearful ire.
Whose music when the earth was born rolled forth,
Sounding in mighty strains in honor of her birth,
And in grand volumes, through the centuries.
Unending sounds; a voice that never dies,
But speaks out from the dawning of the world
Until the earth is dead.—
There was a battle that my soul did love;
The grand old ocean never wearying,
But sending still its billows 'gainst the earth.

    Hela. And I remember how the ships sailed on,
Their sails like specks upon the dark horizon;
And how you told me of the sea king's deeds.

    Ehrens. And that I, too, when grown to be a man,
Would own a ship and live amid the storms;
For then I loved to see the sky grow black,
And hear the rumbling of the distant storms;
To see the white waves breaking on the ocean,
And watch the lightning glide across the heaven;
I loved to hear the distant rolling thunder,
And guide my bark across the raging sea.
And then I well remember that one time
When, side by side, we stood upon the beach,
I told sweet Hela that I loved her then,
And then she told me that she loved me, too,
And when I now repeat the tale again,
Will Hela tell me she loves me now? [*Takes her in his arms.*
Now all the battle of my life is done.

Enter ROMER.

Romer. 'Tis not yet done, and if you now escape,
Full many a battle for your life shall yet
Loom like a monster in the coming future.
[ROMER and EHRENSVARD draw their swords and commence
to fight; EHRENSVARD has his sword knocked from his hand,
and ROMER is about to run him through, when HELA springs
in front of EHRENSVARD, receives the blow and falls dead.
EHRENSVARD rises.]

Ehrens. Add to your sweet revenge in murdering her
My death.
Add to this glorious deed my piteous life.
Oh what a grand revenge was this one here!
Go hang that bloody sword, a mighty trophy,
Where men in time to come shall see its blood,
The record of your honor!
But first add to this teeming hour
Another deed, and take my life from me.

Romer. It was your worthless life that caused this act;
If you had ne'er existed, then this act
Had ne'er been done.
You were the stumbling-block the gods prepared
For her to fall upon. Since that sole act,
For which you were created, is performed,
Then die; and go and tell them who have made you
Of this damned deed! [*Makes as if he would take his life.*
But no! you still shall live and suffer, and therein
Soothe me in my revenge! Ah, Hela, sweet;
Better a star were blotted from high Heaven
Than you were taken from this earth of ours;—
That all the light that ever filled the world

Were strangled by the dark.   But here's no place
To tell my grief that's more than man e'er felt.
[Enter two of EHRENSVARD's soldiers.]
Ehrens.   Seize on that bloody villain !
[ROMER and the soldiers fight.   EHRENSVARD takes his sword
and goes to their assistance.   ROMER retreats and escapes.]

ACT V.

SCENE I.—The camp of ROMER's army.   Time, night.
ROMER discovered.

Romer.   What are these gloomy thoughts that crowd
   upon me,
Each as th' uncertain shadow of some woe ?
Enter WELHAVEN.
Welhav.   What, not abed ?   And yet the dawn is near.
Romer.   My mind's disturbed, and sleep will not rest
   on it.
Welhav.   What are your thoughts, my lord ?
Romer.   Most weary thoughts ;
My thoughts are like the thoughts of drowning men—
Of all my life that's gone ;—I know not why,
But all the scenes of childhood crowd upon me,
Displacing things more germane to the present.
Welhav.   This comes from having overstrained your
   strength.
Romer.   Do you believe, my lord, there's aught of truth
In these strange premonitions that we have ?
Welhav.   Our learned men tell us, sire, that charlatans
Alone can find conclusions in them.
Romer.   A grave conclusion, coming from grave heads,
And yet I'd fear to risk my hope of Heaven

Solely upon their wisdom.
We 're infants only on our mother earth,
That look with wistful eyes upon her face,
To read her thoughts ; or stare at Heaven
To read the physiognomy of night ;
And as I read, my lord, all's wrote in frowns ,—
A haughty night, that bears an angry brow ;
And all my dreams of late have told disasters
'Till now I dare not sleep.   If I should die,
I wonder what odd libel men would make
Of my poor memory.—I wonder, too,—
Is there a world to come ?

    Enter a scout and several officers.

Scout.   My liege, the bridge over which you intended to cross was borne away by the increased storm.

Romer [*to officer.*]   Order out a hundred pioneers to repair the bridge.

Scout.   It cannot be repaired ; it is borne away entirely.

Romer.   Then we must meet the enemy where we are, unless another crossing can be found.   Has the stream been sounded ?   Is there no ford ?

Scout.   The officer who has sounded the stream sends word that he has found one place where the troops might pass, but as the bottom is rocky and the velocity of the stream much increased, the passage would be dangerous.

Romer.   Where is the ford ?

Scout.   By the three stauled pine trees—three-fourths of a mile from here.

Romer.   The depth of the water ?

Scout.   Near breast deep.

Romer. This ford will be dangerous, but we shall pass it. [*To officer.*] The dawn begins to show. Set our army on the march at once, and see that the men keep their bows in their cases, so that the strings be not wet in the crossing.
[*Exeunt officer and scout. Soldiers heard to march within.*

Romer. Now shall our arrows like a storm of hail
Fall on the foe when they begin to cross,
And by the heavens we'll conquer them to-day.
And you, my officers, I charge you all
To cut each coward to the ground who dares
To turn his back upon the enemy ;
And after we have overcome the Danes
I'll have his body hung upon a tree
That crows may strip the dastard of his flesh.

1st Off. You do your men a wrong my liege.

Romer. If I have done them wrong, let them to-day
Prove by their deeds that I have slandered them.

1st Off. I speak for them, my liege ;—they will.

Romer. Then let us take our places at their head,
And hurry forward to the place of battle,
Where we will wait until the Danes have come,
And then we'll slaughter them until the stream
Swelled by their blood does cast its bloody waters,
With mighty roar downward its rocky way.
[*Exeunt king and officers.*

SCENE II.—Another part of the country. Alarms. Enter the Danish General with several officers.

Gen. [*To first off.*] Take three hundred men from the reserve and hurry to the aid of the left wing, which grows weaker ; and you sir, [*to another officer*] lead your forces

round yonder hill, and come upon the enemy in the rear,
while we will keep his front engaged.   [*Exit 2d officer.*
Now for another charge upon them.   [*Exeunt.*
        Alarms.   Enter KING ROMER, and soldiers.

Romer.   Never again will I speak ill of you,—
When they did throw their hordes of men around you
Nobly you cut your passage through their lines ;—
Now that their lines are broken let us charge them,
And we will drive them from the battle-field.   [*Exeunt.*
        Enter a Danish officer who is followed by soldiers.

Off.   For the love of your country be led by me in another
charge against them.

Sold.   'Tis certain death ; the devil's in this king and
fiends possess his men.

Off.   The king is but a man like yourselves.

Sold.   Then why was he not harmed when he fought
alone in the center of our ranks ?

Off.   Because he fought with cowards.
Villains, you shall stand another charge, and if you flee, it
        shall be over my dead body.

[*Alarms within.   The soldiers rush out pushing the
officers with them.*]
        Enter King ROMER.

Romer.   The enemy is flying in all directions ! Some
follow the rocky beach, and some rush over the mountains
toward their ships.   Come, my men, as yet we have done
nothing.—let's be upon them ; down upon them, down and
forever.   And when they 're conquered, then for the usurper.
                                                [*Exeunt.*

SCENE III.   A street.

Enter NEILSEN and LEOPOLD.

Leo.   Now, like the fox we must hide all our steps
That we did make when Ehrensvard was king ;
Since he has now been driven from the throne,
By the true king, who now is on his throne,
So firmly seated naught can ever move him—

Neil.   But others will inform that we did turn
Against him when the people did rebel—

Leo.   Nay, all are guilty and they dare not speak.

Neil.   And did you note how, when he stormed the city,
How strong the people were for Ehrensvard ;—
How, as he more and more successful grew,
The people more did fall from Ehrensvard ;
And how, when Ehrensvard did sound retreat,
But few did follow him.

Leo.   And now once more he hides back in the moun-
     tains.
With bitter heart waiting for time's revenges.

Neil.   I hear that he had quarreled with Arvicka
Before the king did drive him from the city.

Leo.   Aye, for Arvicka said that Ehrensvard,
Like Romer did oppress the people, too.

Neil.   Well, well, it matters little though to us
What man does rule, for there will always be
Some to oppress, and some to steal from us,
Some to pervert the laws, and some to make
Laws worse than those perverted.
Then let us take the smoothest path of life,
And ever cry for him that holds the power.

Leo.   Which way do you go now ?

Neil.   My way is towards the Palace, there to greet,
My lord, the king.

Leo.   Then I will with you.   [*Exeunt.*

SCENE IV.—A room in the Palace.   In the back part of the room
is a couch with red curtains hanging over it.

Enter two ladies, FRIGA and EMBLA.

Frig.   Hear the night wind, a storm comes from the
        north.
Raging and tearing onward through the heaven.

[*Storms within.*

The heavens are angry and the clouds will shake
A deluge on us ere the morning comes.
I do remember once, long years ago,
A night like this; the sky was dark as pitch,
And through that darkness rushed the loosened winds
Howling destruction as they raced along,
Their tones grew louder and the oak trees moaned,
Beneath the blow each heavy blast laid on,
A lightning flash split through a swollen cloud,
And loosed the rain that poured in torrents down,
The thunder followed and the sounding hills,
Cast back each echo 'gainst the shattered clouds.

Embla.   On such a night, they say the dead arise
Their spirits riding on the midnight storms,
And guiding them on through the seas of darkness.
The night moves onward with a mad career.

[*Wind howls and distant thunder heard.*

Friga.   The storm grows louder; how it howls without :
The heavens grow angry and they rave at earth,
The poor earth trembles fearing heavens roar.

Embla. Hist you, for when the heavens show their
    anger,
'Tis my belief some horrid crime on earth
Will soon be done beneath the heavens eye ;
Some murdered body send a bloody vapor
To float off on the moving atmosphere.
    Friga. Hark ! what was that ?
    Embla. I did hear nothing.
Enter an officer of the king's bed-chamber and two others
            who cross the stage.
    1st. Off. The quartered moon is down,
And all the star-lit candles of the night
Were long ago blown out.
    2d Off. A fearful night—
    3d Off. There'll be damage before the morning.
                         [Exeunt.

    Friga. I wonder is there any mortal out
To battle 'gainst the raging elements ?—
I well remember once long years ago—
    Embla. My frighted soul does flit about my body
Like a poor bird that seeks a hiding place ;
A fearful feeling now steals over me,
As if it did fortell some dreadful horror.—
Hark how the thunder rattles near and far !
Some heavy battlement of heaven's down
And thunder leaping o 'er the walls of heaven—
             Enter the king.
    Romer. Ha ! dost hear the storm !
The whole world rots, and rotting thunders burst,
And your sweet faces ladies, too, must—
Why bless you all must rot, rot, rot,

Villians and angels, saints and sinners
Must all come to it—
   Ladies.   Good night to you my lord.   [*Exeunt ladies.*
   Romer.   Oh wretched life; the haven of weariness,
The harbor for a thousand passing ills,
Pain's dwelling place ; the home of misery,
The battleground where sickness and where woe
Do strive for mastery.   I'm weary of it,—
Is there no place where all this rush of life—
This tumult, and this everlasting roar
Does cease forever ?   Aye, that place is death.
Well, well, I must wait its coming,
My stormy heart is broke ; and like a child,
I 'm meek and gentle as a lamb is now.
Enter the QUEEN.   Her eyes are sunken and her face is pale,
    as if from a long illness.   ROMER gazes steadily upon
    her for some moments.
   Romer.   What's this?   I had forgot ;—nay, 'twas a
    dream,
And in that dream I thought that you were dead.
I saw you sleeping with your grave companions ;
On either side I saw the slimy worms
Lay coiled in sleep ; and in those sockets,
Where once your bright eyes gleamed,
They lay at rest.   I heard the midnight winds
Creep o'er your grave ; and saw the sickly moon
Smile through the trees and down on your white tomb—
   Queen.   A pretty dream; would that the dream were true!
But in this dreary night God's eloquence
Heard in the solemn thunder, has awaked
Those thoughts of mine that your harsh cruelty

Had put to sleep ; so that their dreams
Filled all my brain with naught but madness.
Up in my lonely room this night
I've seen most hideous sights, which all foretold
The nearness of your death.   I watched these scenes until
They grew in size and number to such proportions
I had not courage left to wait the end.
Standing upon the bosom of the night,
Dark shadows drawn around her,
Her white face colored by the moon's dim light,
I saw the face of Hela.   She pointed downward
With warning finger, here, to where you are,
And then moved on.   Next came a headless corpse
And in its arms it bore a bloody head
Severed by your command ; and it moved on,
A mother came on next, and in her arms
She bore a child ; and all his curly locks
Reeked with that blood that from his youthful veins
Had poured at your command.   And walking still
A long train passed me by of gory figures,
And each one as he passed did point
To where you stand.   And in the night without
I heard the while their dismal hollow voices,
That mingled with the wind,
And which were hushed oft by the loud-mouthed thunder,
Pronounce your death.   And still this strange procession,
Shown by the lightning's glare, the moon's pale beam,
Moved onward.
    Romer.   Were I a child, these tales might make me
        quake,
But when I grew a man I banished fear.

Though 1 have lined the harsh path of my life
With wrongful deeds for monuments,
When I am dead, I now fear death no more.

    [A shriek heard within. Exit queen.

Murder is loose and mingles with the storm ;
All nature is convulsed and writhes with pain—
So I must die !   A grand deed is 't to die ;
And yet the very dogs perform the deed.
And must I fear when I perform the act ?
I die each hour, and should I live to-morrow
To-night were dead.   Aye, and that very to-morrow
Teems with as much uncertainty
As realms beyond the grave.
I'll be no coward then, but with a heart
Steeled up to high adventure,
With dauntless front, go like a conqueror
To tread the world beyond !
My eyelids droop ; my weary frame needs sleep ;
There 's music in the angry voice of nature
Will soothe me.

[*He lies down on a couch in the back part of the room. A*
 bell tolls without. A moment after enter Ehrensvard.

 Ehrens. My rise was but to make my fall a curse ;
And from a king I am become an assassin.
Yet a bitter hate is in my heart,
That drives soft sleep from out my brain at night,
And in the day does make my brain afire.
That which I've striven for many and many a year for,
Those fondest hopes that time has built in me,—
This man has made them all a fallen ruin.
The only sweet thing that he leaves me now

Is swift revenge.   [*He walks up to the couch.*
Those eyes shall sleep another sleep soon now,
And that pale face shall take a paler hue.
Now for the stroke ; now let his red blood flow ;—
'Twould run down to the floor ; that cheek is pale—
'Tis pale, 'tis very pale.—Hark ! How the thunder rolls,—
Crash ! crash ! crash ! 'tis rolling down the heavens.
What ! Who spoke ? A weary, weary face,—
The blood would stream a-down that weary face,
And in his eyes—I cannot do this deed,
My arm grows weak when I would make the stroke ;
This thunder roaring up above my head does seem to speak.
[*Starts to go, when the king wakes, and seeing Ehrensvard
    springs toward him, and is stabbed by him.*]
Romer.   My time has come at last, now I must go
Out in the dark.   Now must I tread that night,
That has no moon ; where never a star is seen ;
Where all the hours that wander on their way
Are robed in darkness.   All my hate has vanished,
Now when I think upon the unseen world.
My bark of death now sails the midnight seas,
To find new worlds.
Hark to the music that does sound my death ;
The mighty music of the thunder-storm ;
The roaring winds the music of the fire,
That in the lightning sounds a half heard note,
And fiends are dancing to the fearful sound ;
I see them gazing through dark clouds around me.
                    Hark ! Hark ! Hark !   [*Dies.*